I0742120

Ric Quintanilla's

How to Catch a Dream

Written and created by

Enrique Quintanilla

Art

Ezequiel Rubio

Dialogs Edited by

Maricela Quintanilla
and Naomi Quintanilla

Copyright © 2024 by Enrique Quintanilla. All rights reserved. Published by Cipher Comics. No part of this publication may be reproduced, distributed, or transmitted in any form or by any means—including photocopying, recording, or other electronic or mechanical methods—without the prior written permission of the author, except as permitted by applicable copyright law. For permission requests, please contact the author at: contact@cipher-comics.com. The story, all names, characters, and incidents portrayed in this work are fictitious. Any resemblance to actual persons (living or deceased), places, buildings, or products is purely coincidental and should not be inferred as intentional.

CONTENTS

FOR MY DAUGHTER, NAOMI.
FOR MY WIFE, CLAUDIA.
AND FOR MY FATHER, "PROFE" ENRIQUE QUINTANILLA (RIP)

I hope you dream, a thousand dreams of me,
all things we've planned, doing together...
TRYING TO DREAM AGAIN?
IT'S GETTING LATE. LET'S GO INSIDE.

I SEE SOMEONE IS NOT VERY CHATTY TODAY.
DID YOU FINISH YOUR LESSONS?
YEAH, I FINISHED THEM EARLIER. WANT TO TAKE A LOOK?
I'VE NEVER LIKED "HYDROSTATICS", THAT BIT ABOUT NOT BEING ABLE TO FIND THE PRESSURE OF...
FLUSHHH
DON'T YOU DARE LAUGH.
HA
HA
HA

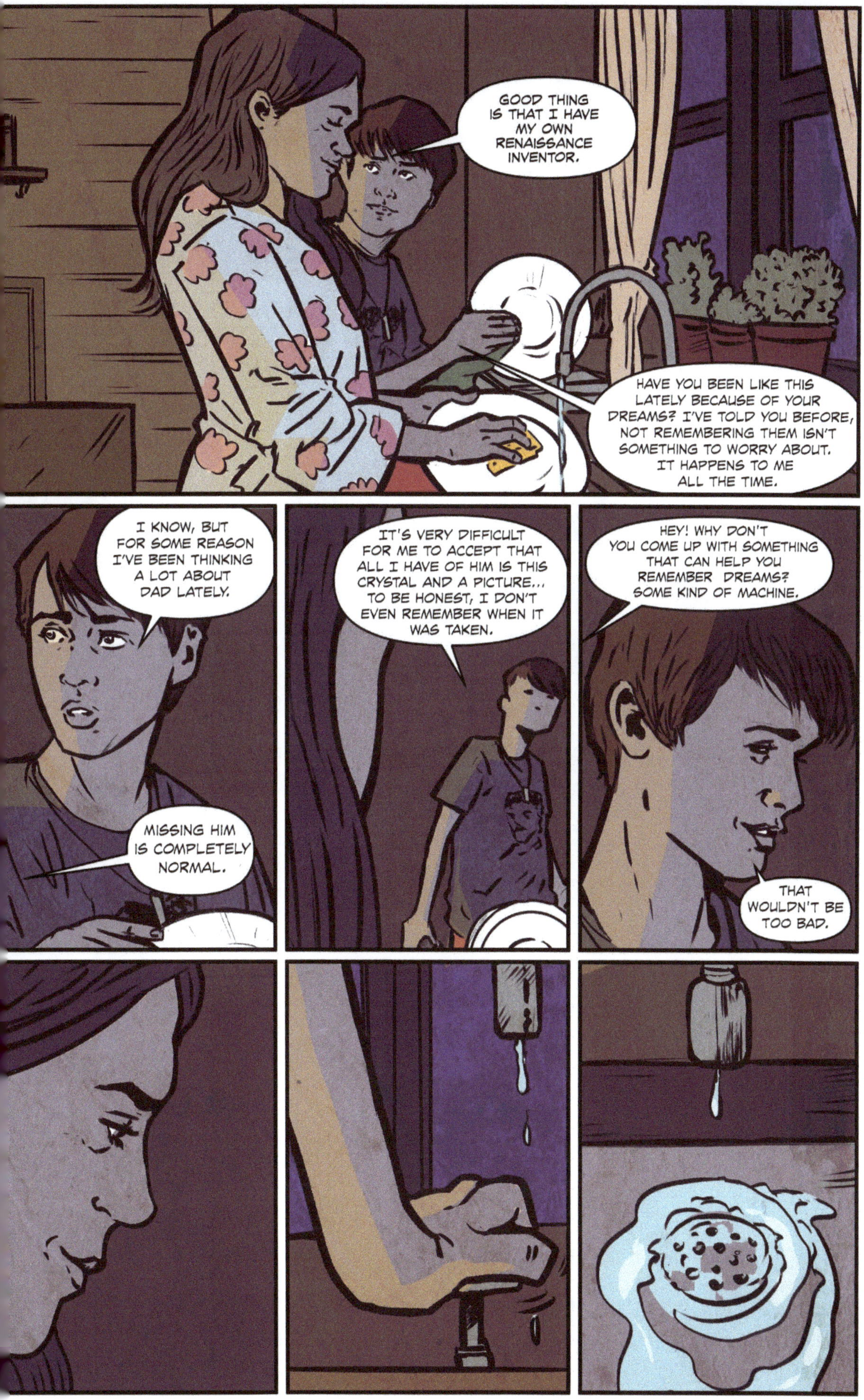
GOOD THING IS THAT I HAVE MY OWN RENAISSANCE INVENTOR.
HAVE YOU BEEN LIKE THIS LATELY BECAUSE OF YOUR DREAMS? I'VE TOLD YOU BEFORE, NOT REMEMBERING THEM ISN'T SOMETHING TO WORRY ABOUT. IT HAPPENS TO ME ALL THE TIME.
I KNOW, BUT FOR SOME REASON I'VE BEEN THINKING A LOT ABOUT DAD LATELY.
MISSING HIM IS COMPLETELY NORMAL.
IT'S VERY DIFFICULT FOR ME TO ACCEPT THAT ALL I HAVE OF HIM IS THIS CRYSTAL AND A PICTURE... TO BE HONEST, I DON'T EVEN REMEMBER WHEN IT WAS TAKEN.
HEY! WHY DON'T YOU COME UP WITH SOMETHING THAT CAN HELP YOU REMEMBER DREAMS? SOME KIND OF MACHINE.
THAT WOULDN'T BE TOO BAD.

NICOLA TESLA
NICOLA TESLA
READY? DID YOU TAKE YOUR PILLS? REMEMBER WHAT WE AGREED ON.
I LOVE YOU. SWEET DREAMS.
YOU TOO, GET SOME REST.. OH, AND BY THE WAY, I LIKE YOUR IDEA.
I KNOW YOU'LL COME UP WITH SOMETHING.
Hold me to your heart
and never let me free
always be close to me
Someday you will find
me in your dreams

GOOD MORNING. YES, WHO'S ASKING? OH, HOW ARE YOU, DIRECTOR?
YES, IT'S BEEN A WHILE. EVERYTHING IS FINE, STILL HERE, I'VE BEEN TAKING CARE OF MY SON...
YEAH... MUCH BETTER, HE MUST STILL BE ON THE BEACH. YES, WE CAN TALK...
...AND THAT'S WHY WE THOUGHT OF YOU. PERSONALLY, I THINK YOU'RE PERFECT FOR THIS NEW POSITION. YOU'VE GOT THE CREDENTIALS AND EXPERIENCE IT REQUIRES.
I DON'T KNOW IF HE IS READY TO GO BACK. IT SOUNDS LIKE A GREAT OPPORTUNITY, AND I LOVE TEACHING, BUT...

SO...DO YOU TAKE IT? BELIEVE ME, IT'S HARD TO FIND SOMEONE WITH A SKILL SET LIKE YOURS.
I REALLY APPRECIATE YOUR OFFER AND TIME. LET ME THINK ABOUT IT THOROUGHLY AND I PROMISE TO CALL YOU BACK AS SOON AS POSSIBLE. IS THAT OKAY?
OKAY, THAT'S FINE, BUT DON'T TAKE TOO LONG. WE'LL BE WAITING FOR YOU.
THANK YOU SO MUCH, HAVE AN EXCELLENT DAY.
YOU'RE NOT GOING TO SAY ANYTHING?
THAT YOU'RE NOT SUPPOSED TO LISTEN TO OTHER PEOPLE'S CONVERSATIONS?
YOU'RE JOKING, RIGHT? CALL THEM BACK RIGHT NOW AND TELL THEM YES!
WHY DON'T WE TALK ABOUT THIS AT ANOTHER TIME?
MOM, WE'LL BE FINE... YOU WILL GO BACK TO DOING WHAT YOU REALLY LOVE, AND I WILL MEET OTHER PEOPLE AND HAVE FRIENDS... FROM ABOVE, I KNOW DAD WILL BE HELPING US.
OK, BUT IF WE DO IT, LET'S DO IT RIGHT, GOT IT? AND FOR THAT, WE NEED YOUR DOCTOR'S APPROVAL.
NO! NO! NOT HIM!

JOURNAL
FLETCHER
EXCUSE ME, MISS. DID YOU INFORM DR. FLETCHER THAT WE ARE WAITING?
YES, MA'AM. THE DOCTOR ALREADY KNOWS. HE WILL SEE YOU AS SOON AS HE IS AVAILABLE
TROUBLE IN PARADISE? I THOUGHT YOU HAD MORE INFLUENCE; WE'VE BEEN SITTING HERE FOR OVER TWO HOURS.

EXCUSE ME, MAYBE...
BRINNG BRINNG
ALRIGHT, DOCTOR, I'LL LET HIM KNOW NOW.
THE DOCTOR SAYS YOU CAN COME IN.
I'M SORRY, THE DOCTOR MENTIONED THAT ONLY THE YOUNG MAN CAN COME IN. IF YOU LIKE, YOU CAN WAIT FOR HIM HERE.
ME? WHAT FOR?

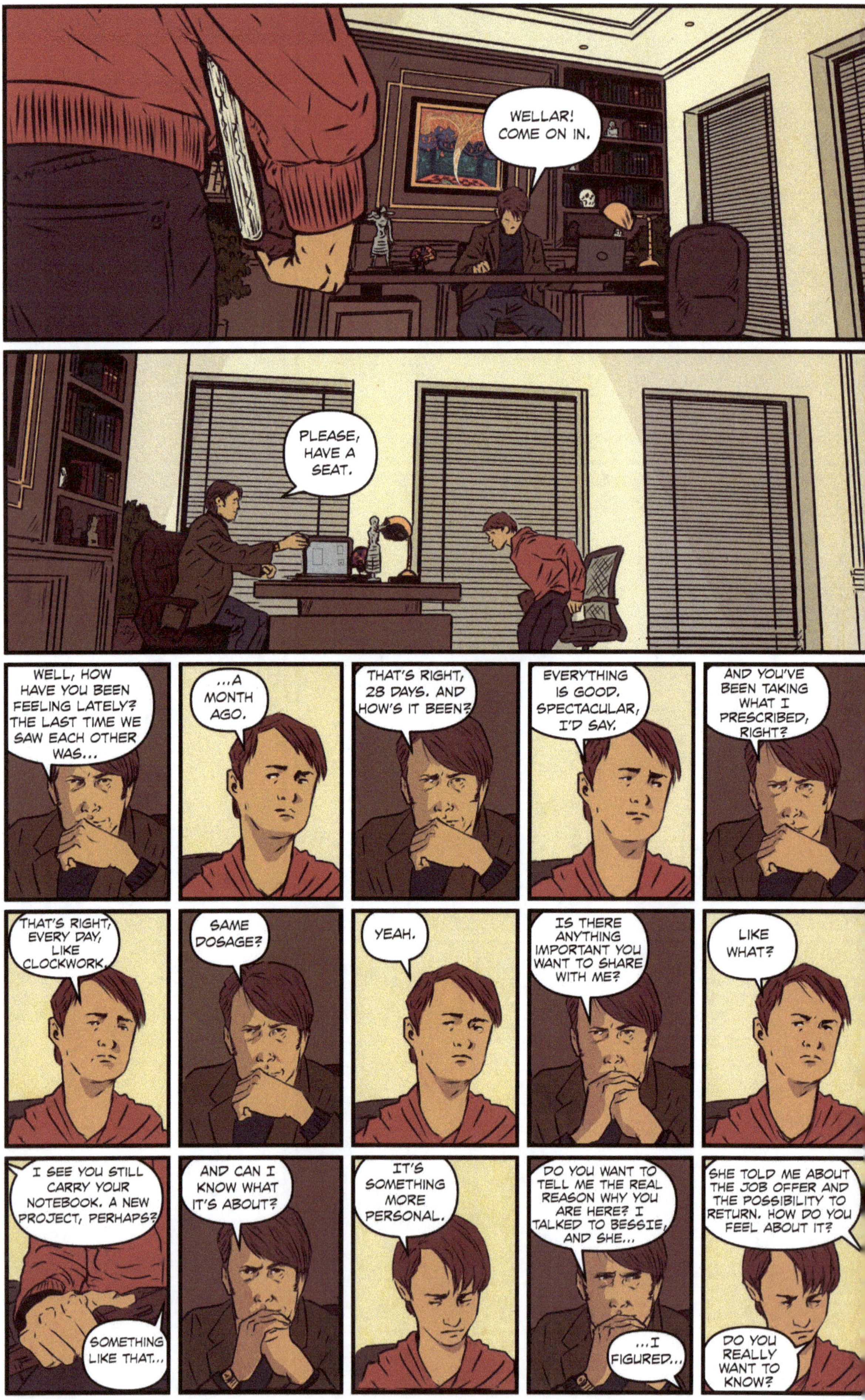
WELLAR! COME ON IN.
PLEASE, HAVE A SEAT.
WELL, HOW HAVE YOU BEEN FEELING LATELY? THE LAST TIME WE SAW EACH OTHER WAS...
...A MONTH AGO.
THAT'S RIGHT, 28 DAYS. AND HOW'S IT BEEN?
EVERYTHING IS GOOD. SPECTACULAR, I'D SAY.
AND YOU'VE BEEN TAKING WHAT I PRESCRIBED, RIGHT?
THAT'S RIGHT, EVERY DAY, LIKE CLOCKWORK.
SAME DOSAGE?
YEAH.
IS THERE ANYTHING IMPORTANT YOU WANT TO SHARE WITH ME?
LIKE WHAT?
I SEE YOU STILL CARRY YOUR NOTEBOOK. A NEW PROJECT, PERHAPS?
SOMETHING LIKE THAT...
AND CAN I KNOW WHAT IT'S ABOUT?
IT'S SOMETHING MORE PERSONAL.
DO YOU WANT TO TELL ME THE REAL REASON WHY YOU ARE HERE? I TALKED TO BESSIE, AND SHE...
...I FIGURED...
SHE TOLD ME ABOUT THE JOB OFFER AND THE POSSIBILITY TO RETURN. HOW DO YOU FEEL ABOUT IT?
DO YOU REALLY WANT TO KNOW?

WELLAR, I'M NOT CLAUDIUS.
WHAT ARE YOU TALKING ABOUT?
I KNOW YOU DISAPPROVE OF MY RELATIONSHIP WITH BESSIE, BUT YOU NEED TO PUT ALL OF THAT ASIDE FOR NOW. DO YOU TRULY WANT ME TO SAY YOU'RE READY TO RETURN?
TO BE HONEST, YES, I FEEL MUCH BETTER AND I THINK...
IF SO, YOU HAVE TO PROVE IT. I MUST BE CERTAIN THAT YOU ARE READY, AND RIGHT NOW, YOUR ATTITUDE IS NOT HELPING MUCH.
THE THING IS...
...I'LL TELL YOU WHAT'S HAPPENING: YOU THINK YOU'RE READY, BUT YOUR MOTHER IS TRYING TO PROTECT YOU. SHE'D DO ANYTHING FOR YOU, SO LET ME ASK YOU AGAIN, WHY ARE YOU HERE?
ALRIGHT, THIS TIME IT SEEMS YOU'RE RIGHT. I'VE BEEN FEELING GREAT THESE PAST FEW MONTHS, AND I HAVE BEEN FOLLOWING YOUR INSTRUCTIONS. BUT I ALSO WANT TO GO OUT, MEET PEOPLE, AND MAKE NEW FRIENDS.
AND IF I HAVE TO GET MORE TESTS DONE, I'M UP FOR WHATEVER YOU SAY. I REALLY WANT TO DO THIS.
YOU ARE REALLY GOOD!
THANKS.
AND WHAT KIND OF DEVICE IS THIS?
IT'S JUST A SKETCH; I'M NOT SURE YET.
DOES THIS HAVE ANYTHING TO DO WITH REMEMBERING YOUR DREAM?
I SEE YOU'RE WELL INFORMED.
YES, PLEASE TELL MRS. BESSIE SHE CAN COME IN.
click

MAINTAIN THE SAME DOSAGE, AND I WANT TO SEE YOU HERE IN TWO WEEKS.
THE GOOD THING IS THAT THE TRIP WILL BE SHORTER. YOU CAN START PACKING TODAY.
AND PLEASE, AT THE FIRST SYMPTOM, LET ME KNOW IMMEDIATELY.
YEAH, DON'T WORRY ABOUT IT; I'LL LET YOU KNOW IF SOMETHING ISN'T RIGHT.
BESIDES, THAT WAY WE CAN SEE EACH OTHER MORE OFTEN, RIGHT?
THANK YOU SO MUCH!
I THINK THAT'S ALL FOR NOW. ANY QUESTIONS?

WELLAR! GOOD LUCK WITH YOUR NEW INVENTION. IT'S GOOD TO FOLLOW YOUR DREAMS.
YOU KNOW WHAT? MAYBE IT WILL HELP ME DISCOVER WHETHER SOMETHING IS STILL ROTTEN IN THE STATE OF DENMARK.

89.5
FM
"We'll be swinging up in dreamland
All night, baby
Where the little cherubs trot"
ISN'T THERE ANYTHING NEWER ON THE RADIO?
I DON'T KNOW, MAYBE...
I HAVE A PLASTIC BAG, IN CASE YOU FEEL SICK.
I'M NOT FIVE ANYMORE.
DON'T YOU WANT ME TO TURN ON THE AC?
DON'T YOU DARE!
OH, AND THANKS FOR BEING NICE TO FLETCHER YESTERDAY.
IT'S NOT LIKE I HAD A CHOICE.

I KNOW WHAT YOU THINK ABOUT HIM, BUT HE'S A GOOD PERSON.
DID YOU TELL HIM SOMETHING ABOUT MY NEW PROJECT?
ABOUT YOUR PROJECT? NO, NOT THAT I CAN RECALL.
IF ONLY YOU GAVE HIM A CHANCE...
MOM, I REALLY DON'T WANT TO TALK ABOUT IT RIGHT NOW. LET ME ENJOY THIS SMALL VICTORY.
SOMETIMES YOU LOOK SO MUCH LIKE YOUR FATHER.
AND HOW WOULD I KNOW? YOU NEVER TALK ABOUT HIM.
AND NOW THAT WE ARE TALKING ABOUT OPTIONS, WHAT HAVE YOU THOUGHT? ARTS OR SCIENCE?
I CAN'T SEE HOW ONE COULD LIVE WITHOUT THE OTHER. I STILL DON'T KNOW.
THE GOOD THING IS THAT YOU STILL HAVE TIME.
DID YOU SEE THOSE CARS AT THE SIDE OF THE ROAD? I THINK THEY'RE WATCHING US.
WATCHING US? YOU'RE IMAGINING THINGS! AND WHO WOULD WANT TO WATCH US?
LOOK, JUST LIKE THAT ONE HAS BEEN FOLLOWING US.
NOW THEY'RE FOLLOWING US?

I'M NOT JOKING AROUND, SEE THAT CAR? DON'T TURN AROUND!
OKAY, OKAY, WHICH CAR? THE ONE THAT PUT ON ITS TURN SIGNAL?
AND WHO DO YOU THINK COULD BE FOLLOWING US?
NEVER MIND.
DID YOU BRING YOUR PILLS?
ANYWAY, WE AREN'T FAR FROM THE HOUSE.
I THOUGHT IT WAS CLOSER TO THE CITY.
YOU DON'T REMEMBER ANYTHING, RIGHT? YOU WERE SO SMALL... I HONESTLY DON'T THINK IT WAS A GOOD IDEA TO COME BACK THERE. WE COULD RENT AN APARTMENT CLOSER TO YOUR SCHOOL.
NO WAY!
OKAY, I JUST THINK THIS IS A "LITTLE" TOO BIG FOR US.

DID YOU SAY A "LITTLE"? THIS IS AMAZING!

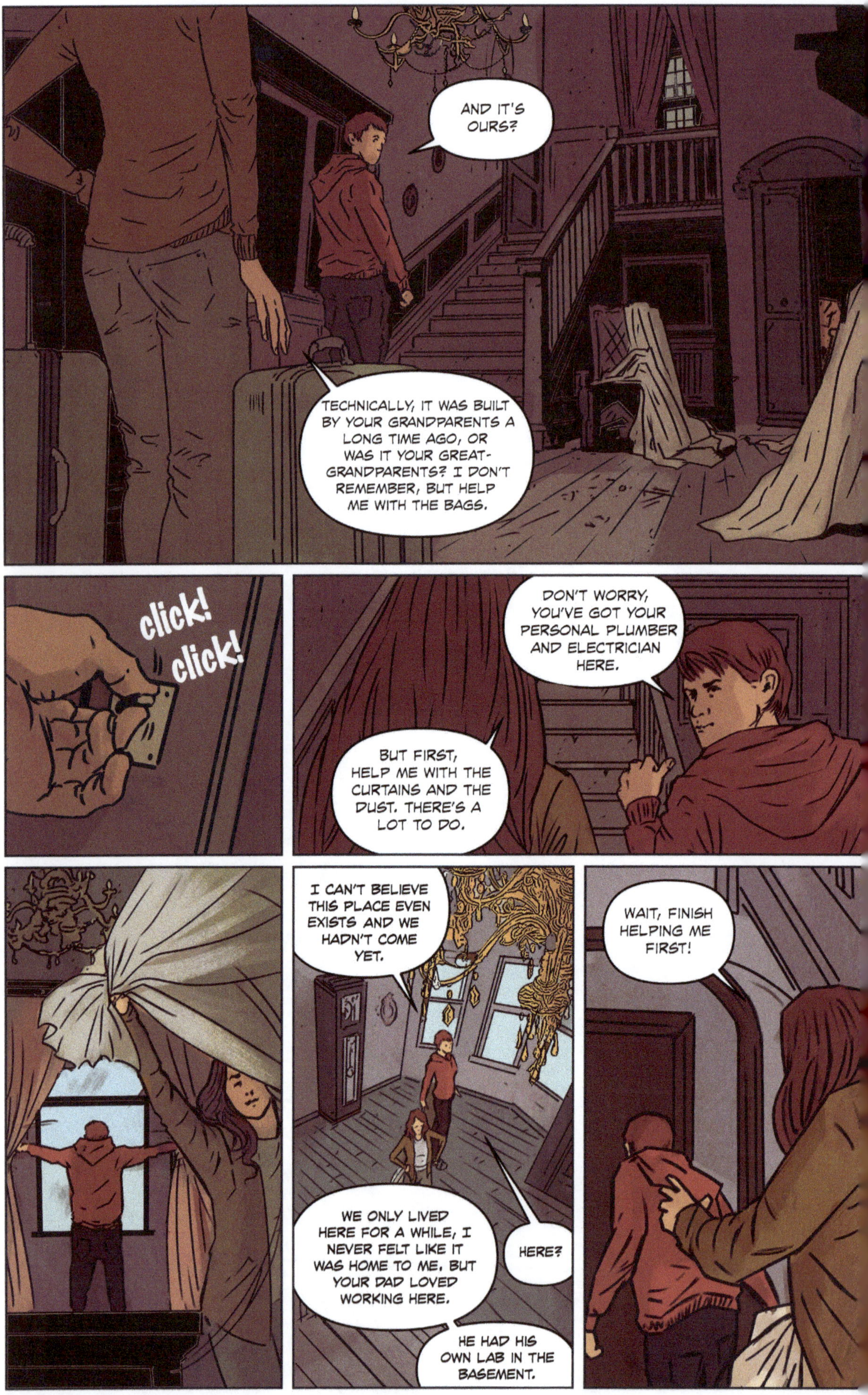
AND IT'S OURS?
TECHNICALLY, IT WAS BUILT BY YOUR GRANDPARENTS A LONG TIME AGO, OR WAS IT YOUR GREAT-GRANDPARENTS? I DON'T REMEMBER, BUT HELP ME WITH THE BAGS.
click! click!
DON'T WORRY, YOU'VE GOT YOUR PERSONAL PLUMBER AND ELECTRICIAN HERE.
BUT FIRST, HELP ME WITH THE CURTAINS AND THE DUST. THERE'S A LOT TO DO.
I CAN'T BELIEVE THIS PLACE EVEN EXISTS AND WE HADN'T COME YET.
WE ONLY LIVED HERE FOR A WHILE, I NEVER FELT LIKE IT WAS HOME TO ME. BUT YOUR DAD LOVED WORKING HERE.
HERE?
HE HAD HIS OWN LAB IN THE BASEMENT.
WAIT, FINISH HELPING ME FIRST!

click!
MAYBE YOU WERE HOPING TO FIND SOMETHING ELSE, BUT THE COLLEGE TOOK EVERYTHING, I'M SORRY.
IT'S PERFECT! CAN YOU SMELL THE SAME THING I DO?
OISTURE?
POTENTIAL...
YOU CAN DEVELOP ITS POTENTIAL LATER. FOR NOW, HELP ME CLEAN UP.
HEY!
THEN HURRY UP!

THIS IS SOMETHING I DIDN'T MISS.
DON'T EVEN LOOK AT ME.
BEEEP! BEEEP!
DOING THAT DOESN'T MAKE YOU GO ANY FASTER.
IF ONLY WE HAD RENTED THE APARTMENT, AS I SUGGESTED.
THAT TOPIC IS OFF THE TABLE. MAYBE IT'S JUST A CAR ACCIDENT AHEAD.

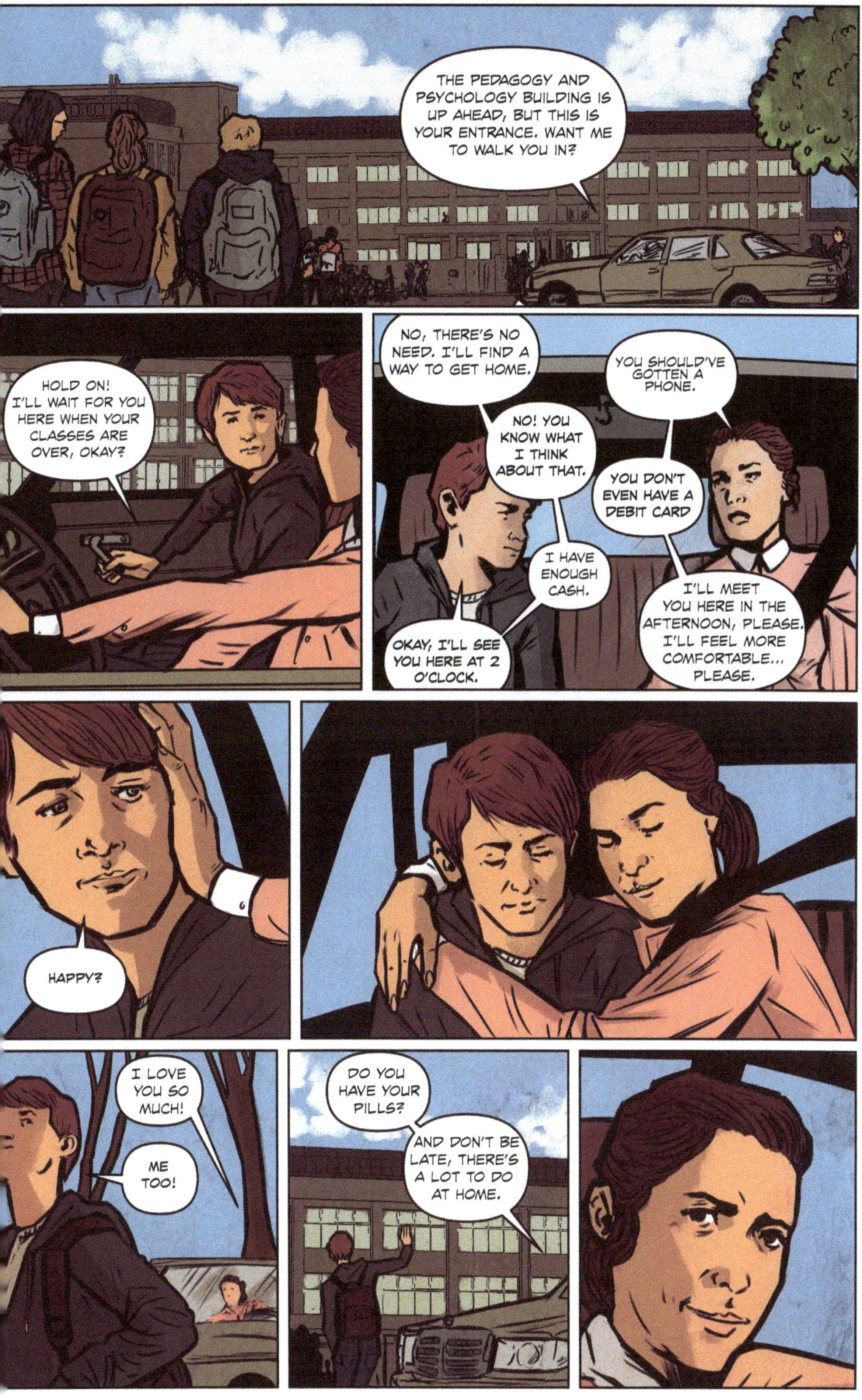
THE PEDAGOGY AND PSYCHOLOGY BUILDING IS UP AHEAD, BUT THIS IS YOUR ENTRANCE. WANT ME TO WALK YOU IN?
HOLD ON! I'LL WAIT FOR YOU HERE WHEN YOUR CLASSES ARE OVER, OKAY?
NO, THERE'S NO NEED. I'LL FIND A WAY TO GET HOME.
YOU SHOULD'VE GOTTEN A PHONE.
NO! YOU KNOW WHAT I THINK ABOUT THAT.
YOU DON'T EVEN HAVE A DEBIT CARD
I HAVE ENOUGH CASH.
I'LL MEET YOU HERE IN THE AFTERNOON, PLEASE. I'LL FEEL MORE COMFORTABLE... PLEASE.
OKAY, I'LL SEE YOU HERE AT 2 O'CLOCK.
HAPPY?
I LOVE YOU SO MUCH!
ME TOO!
DO YOU HAVE YOUR PILLS?
AND DON'T BE LATE, THERE'S A LOT TO DO AT HOME.

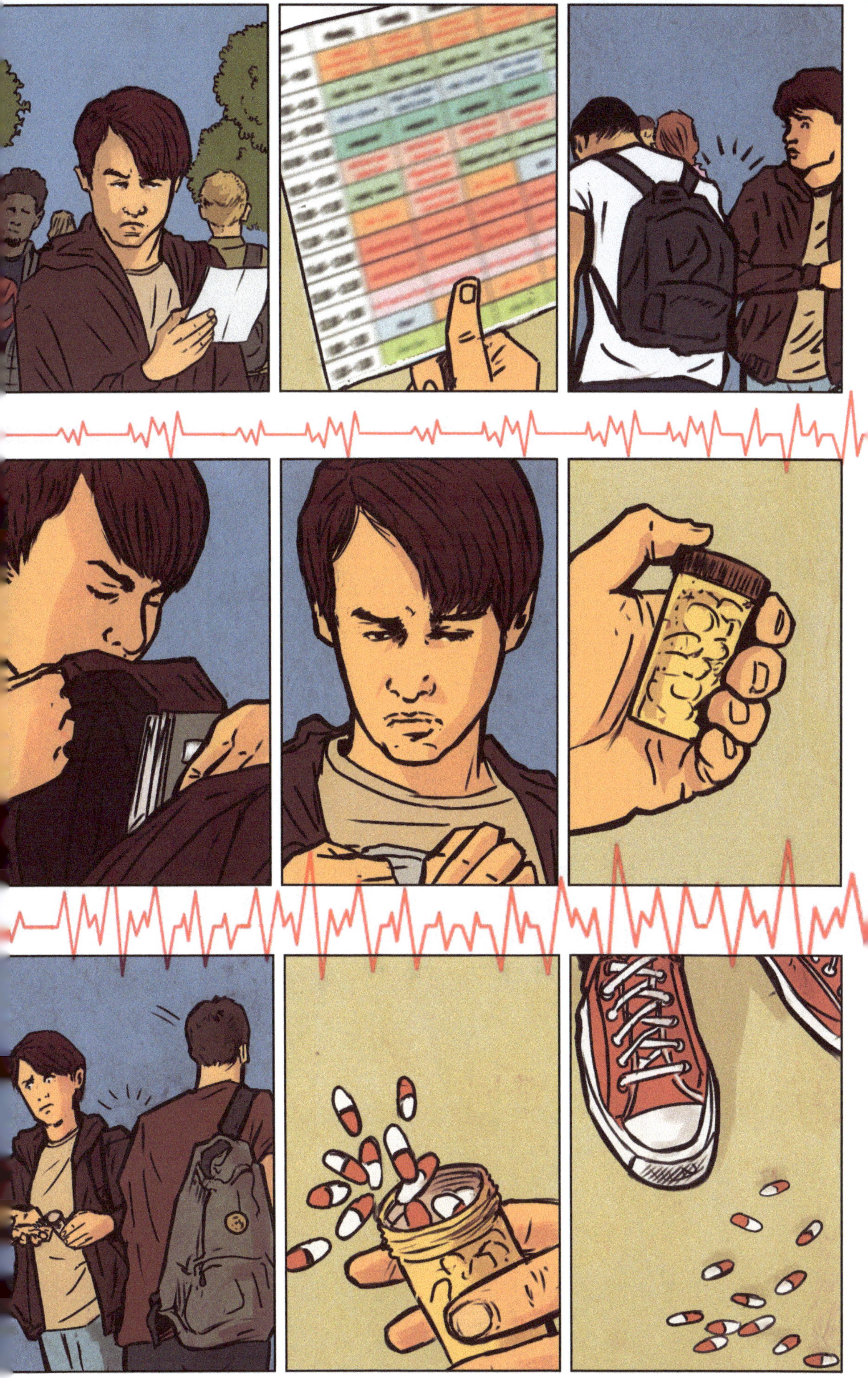

HEY, YOU OKAY, KID?
TO BE CONTINUED...

DREAMBUSTERS
BAND

ARE YOU OK?
...YEAH.
DO YOU NEED ANY HELP?
I'M LOOKING FOR CLASS ROOM 4-307.
IT'S ON THE OTHER SIDE. THIRD BUILDING, FOLLOW THIS SIDEWALK AND YOU'LL GET THERE WITH NO TROUBLE.
THANK YOU SO MUCH!
IS IT YOUR FIRST DAY HERE?
YEAH, YOU CAN TELL, RIGHT?
DON'T WORRY, YOU WILL GET USED TO THIS PLACE IN A COUPLE OF DAYS.
THANK YOU AGAIN.
WHAT'S YOUR NAME KID?
WELLAR, NICE TO MEET YOU
THE PLEASURE IS MINE. YOUR FACE LOOKS FAMILIAR, I DON'T KNOW WHY. WELL, GO ON, IT'S GETTING LATE. AND DON'T HESITATE TO ASK ME IF YOU NEED ANY HELP.
WILL DO!

WELL? ARE YOU COMING IN?
MATH?
YOU TELL ME. DOES IT LOOK LIKE "SHORTHAND" TO YOU?
UP FRONT. I DON'T BITE.
YOUR NAME?
WELLAR.
NOT A VERY COMMON NAME. TRANSFER FROM ANOTHER SCHOOL?
KIND OF.
WHAT DO YOU WANT ME TO DO?
SOLVE IT?
GO AHEAD.

IF IT COULD BE SOLVED, SURE, BUT THE EQUATION IS MIS-FORMULATED.
IT'S INCONSISTENT, AND THE RESULTING LINES WOULD BE PARALLEL.
HOWEVER, IF WE MODIFY THIS PART AND SUBSTITUTE THERE...
...THE SOLUTION MIGHT BE "3X9Y12Z", AS LONG AS WE SUBSTITUTE THE VARIABLES BEFORE WE START ISOLATING.
YOU CAN GO AND SIT IN THE BACK, HOPEFULLY SOMEONE LEARNED SOMETHING.
DID ANYBODY UNDERSTAND WHAT YOUR CLASSMATE SAID? NOBODY? ALL RIGHT, THAT'S THE HOMEWORK FOR TOMORROW.

WELLAR! WELLAR!
FINALLY! I THOUGHT I'D NEVER CATCH UP TO YOU. BADASS MOVE BACK THERE, THAT JERK THOUGHT HE COULD MESS WITH YOU. I CAN'T STAND HIM.
THANKS?
I'M SHEP.
WELLAR.
I KNOW. LET ME SEE YOUR SCHEDULE... YOU'RE LUCKY, WE HAVE PRETTY MUCH THE SAME CLASSES.
YEP, IT'S ALMOST IDENTICAL TO MINE. SO, WHERE ARE WE MEETING TO DO THE HOMEWORK?
LAST CLASS IS AT 2 PM. WE CAN GO TO A PARK. YOU DOWN?
I'M DOWN.
I CAN'T, I HAVE STUFF TO DO AT HOME, AND MY MOM WILL PICK ME UP AT THE PARKING LOT.
THEN, LET'S GO TO YOUR PLACE, WE CAN HELP.
AWESOME! WHAT'S YOUR NUMBER?
MY NUMBER?
YOUR PHONE NUMBER, CELLPHONE.
I DON'T HAVE ONE.
REALLY? THAT'S ODD. WHY?
WHAT DO YOU MEAN WHY? THE "ALGORITHM".
WHAT ABOUT IT?
IT KNOWS WHERE YOU ARE, WHAT YOU SAY, WHAT YOU DO, AND...
...WHATEVER YOU'RE THINKING?
WELL, THAT ALGORITHM CAN KISS MY A@@.

SO SORRY, I HAD TO STAY FOR A FEW MORE MINUTES.
IT'S FINE, IT'S NOT A BIG DEAL.
I PROMISE...
...I SAID THAT IT'S FINE.
WELL, ARE YOU READY?
JUST ONE THING: A COUPLE OF FRIENDS ARE COMING OVER, THEY CAN HELP US CLEAN. IS THAT OKAY?
FRIENDS?
GOOD AFTERNOON MA'AM.
HI!
HI...I'M BESSIE.
DO YOU WANT TO GRAB A FEW PIZZAS FIRST?

WELCOME HOME!
PIZZA
WHERE DO YOU WANT TO START?
HONESTLY, I THOUGHT THAT IT WAS JUST LIKE CLEANING YOUR ROOM.
SERVES YOU RIGHT, BIG MOUTH.
WE CAN START DOWN HERE, AND THEN MOVE TO THE BASEMENT. THERE'S A LOT OF ROOM THERE TO DO THE HOMEWORK.
WELL, IT'S NOT LIKE I HAVE A CHOICE, RIGHT?

...AND THIS WOULD BE THE FINAL SOLUTION, IT'S RELATIVELY SIMPLE.
LET ME SEE, I BETTER TAKE A PICTURE.
WEIRD, I DON'T HAVE A SIGNAL.
BUT, DID YOU UNDERSTAND IT?
DO YOU HAVE A GAME CONSOLE?
DO YOU SEE A TV ANYWHERE?
AND THIS THING? DOES IT WORK?
TO BE HONEST, I HAVEN'T TRIED IT. WE BARELY GOT HERE YESTERDAY.
IF WE EVER WANTED TO GO TO THE BEACH WHERE YOU USED TO LIVE, DO YOU THINK WE COULD STAY THERE A FEW DAYS?
I THINK SO.
COOL!
WELL, IT DEFINITELY DOESN'T WORK.
I NEED TO TAKE A LOOK AT IT.
ANYWAY, IT'S ALL SUPER OLD SONGS.
I GUESS IT WAS MY DAD'S.
YOU GUESS? WHY DON'T YOU ASK HIM?
HE'S NO LONGER WITH US. HE PASSED AWAY SEVERAL YEARS AGO.
I'M SO SORRY.
WHAT DID HE DIE OF?
IT'S NONE OF YOUR BUSINESS!

ALL I KNOW IS THAT THERE WAS AN ACCIDENT. MY MOM'S NEVER TOLD ME EXACTLY WHAT HAPPENED, SHE ALWAYS AVOIDS THE TOPIC.
LOOKS LIKE THIS WAS HIS WORKPLACE, SOME KIND OF LAB.
REALLY?
I'M DOWN!
WE CAN HELP YOU FIGURE IT OUT. SHEP'S GREAT AT DIGGING AROUND ONLINE, HE'S KIND OF A GEEK, AND I KNOW A BUNCH OF PEOPLE AND PLACES.
ARE YOU DOWN?
AREN'T WE?
WE'RE HEADING OUT, THE ROAD'S LONG.
I CAN ASK MOM TO TAKE YOU HOME.
NO WAY! WE'LL TAKE A CAB. ELLA LIVES CLOSE TO MY PLACE.
BE THERE EARLY TOMORROW MORNING, WE HAVE "TECHNICAL DRAWING" CLASS, AND THE TEACHER IS VERY STRICT.
YEAH, I KNOW WHERE THE CLASSROOM IS.
BUILDING NUMBER 3, THE LAST ROOM ON THE HALL. BE THERE BEFORE 7, OTHERWISE, THE DOOR WILL BE CLOSED.
SINCE WE'RE ALL BEING NOSY, WHAT'S THAT NOTEBOOK YOU CARRY EVERYWHERE FOR?
I'M MAKING ANNOTATIONS FOR A PROJECT I'M WORKING ON.
COOL! WHAT IS THIS PROJECT ABOUT?
IT'S A LONG STORY. I'LL TELL YOU ANOTHER DAY.
WELL, GOODBYE, WE ALREADY KNOW THE WAY OUT.
SEE YOU TOMORROW!
DON'T BE LATE!
Schhhhh

IS IT A BAD TIME?
NO, OF COURSE NOT.
I HAVE TO SAY, I'M AMAZED AT HOW FAST YOU MADE NEW FRIENDS. I'M HAPPY AND VERY PROUD OF YOU.
DON'T STAY UP LATE.
I'LL JUST TIDY UP HERE AND GO TO BED.
YOUR DAD LOVED THAT KIND OF MUSIC. HOPEFULLY YOU CAN GET IT WORKING. OH, AND YOU KNOW WHAT? I REMEMBER IT USED TO BE ON THE OTHER SIDE, I DON'T KNOW WHO MOVED IT.

...SO DREAM, WHEN THE DAY IS THROUGH...
...DREAM, AND THEY MIGHT COME TRUE...
...THINGS NEVER ARE AS BAD AS THEY SEEM...
...SO DREAM, DREAM, DREAM!
CLICK!

PLUFF!

TECHNICAL 7:00
DRAWING
YOU BARELY MADE IT.
I OVERSLEPT.
WE CAN TELL.
OPEN YOUR BOOK TO PAGE 42. THAT'S THE FIGURE YOU HAVE TO DRAW, IN ALL ITS VIEWS. IF YOU DON'T HAVE THE BOOK ASK A CLASSMATE. YOU MUST FINISH WITHIN THE CLASS TIME.
AND REMEMBER: "A+" IS FOR GOD, "A" IS FOR ME, AND WE'LL TAKE IT FROM THERE. DON'T RAISE YOUR VOICE. PLEASE WRITE YOUR NAME AND DATE, OTHERWISE, IT'S AN "F".
I CAN LEND YOU THE BOOK FOR A FEW MINUTES.
NO, IT'S OKAY.

07:05
07:15
ARE YOU DONE?
YEAH.
NEXT CLASS I'LL BE GIVING THE GRADES.
ANY OTHER DA VINCI ALREADY FINISHED?

C-24
WHY DID YOU TAKE SO LONG? I'VE BEEN WAITING FOR YOU.
WE'RE ALREADY HERE. WHAT'S UP?
DO YOU STILL WANT TO HELP ME OUT WITH MY RESEARCH?
WHAT DO YOU MEAN BY "STILL"? OF COURSE!
I'LL NEED YOUR HELP, BUT I HAVE SOMETHING TO SHOW YOU FIRST. HOW ABOUT WE GO TO THE LIBRARY?
LIBRARY? NOBODY GOES THERE ANYMORE. TELL ME WHAT I NEED TO RESEARCH AND I'LL FIND IT IN A FLASH.
I DON'T THINK YOU WILL FIND ANYTHING THERE.
DON'T SAY IT'S BECAUSE OF THE FU@@@NG ALGORITHM.
I'M TELLING YOU WE DON'T NEED TO GO THERE. JUST TELL ME WHAT YOU NEED TO KNOW, AND I BET YOU I CAN FIND IT...

...AND THESE ARE THE SYMBOLS I WAS ABLE TO DRAW. IT WAS A MATTER OF SECONDS.
BUT, CAN YOU MAKE THEM APPEAR AGAIN?
NOT YET, I TRIED ALL NIGHT.
MAYBE IT WAS JUST A DREAM.
THAT'S IMPOSSIBLE.
WHY IS IT IMPOSSIBLE?
OKAY, I'LL TELL YOU SOMETHING... I DON'T DREAM.
C'MON! EVERYBODY DREAMS!
SHHH!!!
PERHAPS YOU DREAM BUT YOU CAN'T REMEMBER. HAVE YOU TRIED HYPNOSIS?
YES, I'VE TRIED EVERYTHING. I EVEN WEAR THIS CRYSTAL ALL THE TIME. IT WAS MY DAD'S, AND IT'S SUPPOSED TO HELP ME REMEMBER MY DREAMS.
IS IT THE ONE YOU USED LAST NIGHT?

YEAH. BUT I NEED TO KNOW EXACTLY WHAT HAPPENED TO MY DAD AND WHAT THOSE SYMBOLS MEAN. I THINK THEY'RE CONNECTED, LIKE HE'S TRYING TO SEND ME A MESSAGE. ARE YOU IN?
DAMN, DUDE!
SHHH!!!
THAT'S HEAVY. I'VE ONLY KNOWN YOU A COUPLE OF DAYS, BUT YOU'RE MY ONLY CHANCE TO PASS MATH.
AND I DON'T HAVE ANYTHING ELSE TO DO, SO... I'M DOWN!
SHHH!!!
IT'S ALMOST 2 O'CLOCK, I'M GOING TO CHECK OUT A FEW BOOKS AND READ THEM AT HOME, WANT TO JOIN ME?
SO DO I. I HAVE TO BE AT HOME, AND THERE'S A CHANCE OF A STORM TONIGHT.
I CAN'T TODAY, I HAVE STUFF TO DO WITH MY PARENTS.
IT IS WHAT IT IS, SEE YOU TOMORROW!

I HATE THUNDER!
KABOOM!!
IS IT GOOD?
MMMHHH.
HOW WAS YOUR DAY. DID YOU SEE YOUR FRIENDS?
IT WAS FINE, YES, WE HUNG OUT IN THE LIBRARY.
I ASSUME THAT'S WHERE YOU GOT ALL THESE BOOKS FROM.
YEAH, IT'S FOR THE PROJECT.
AND HOW'S IT GOING?
I HAVE A FEW IDEAS, BUT NOTHING SOLID YET.
ARE YOU GOING TO HELP ME WITH THE DISHES TONIGHT?
SORRY, I HAVE A LOT OF HOMEWORK, I'LL GO TO THE BASEMENT AND FROM THERE TO BED.
WELLAR? IF THERE'S SOMETHING ELSE YOU'D TELL ME, RIGHT?
OF COURSE!
KABOOM!!

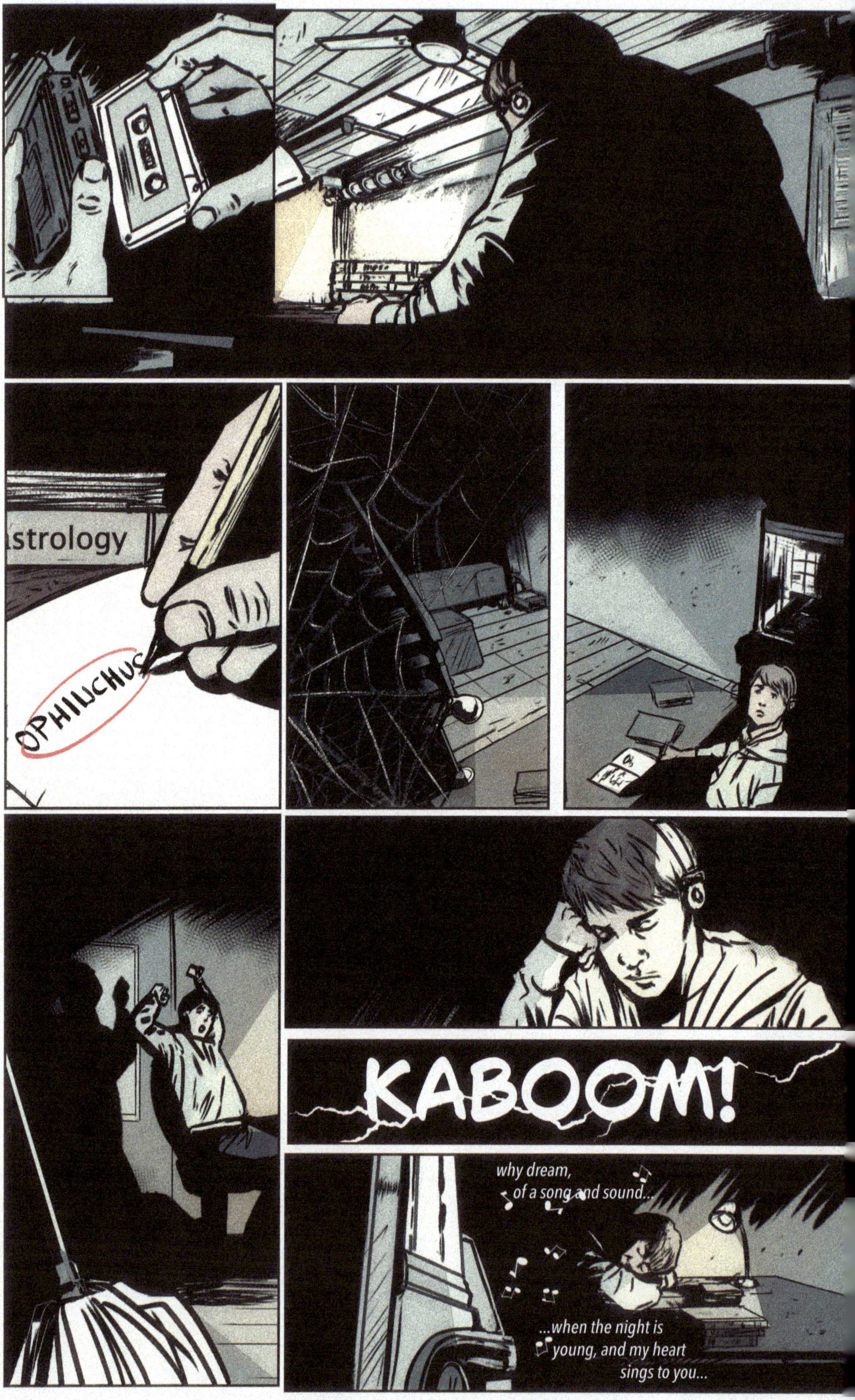
astrology
OPHIUCHUS
KABOOM!
why dream,
of a song and sound...
...when the night is
young, and my heart
sings to you...

KAABOOM
KAABOOM

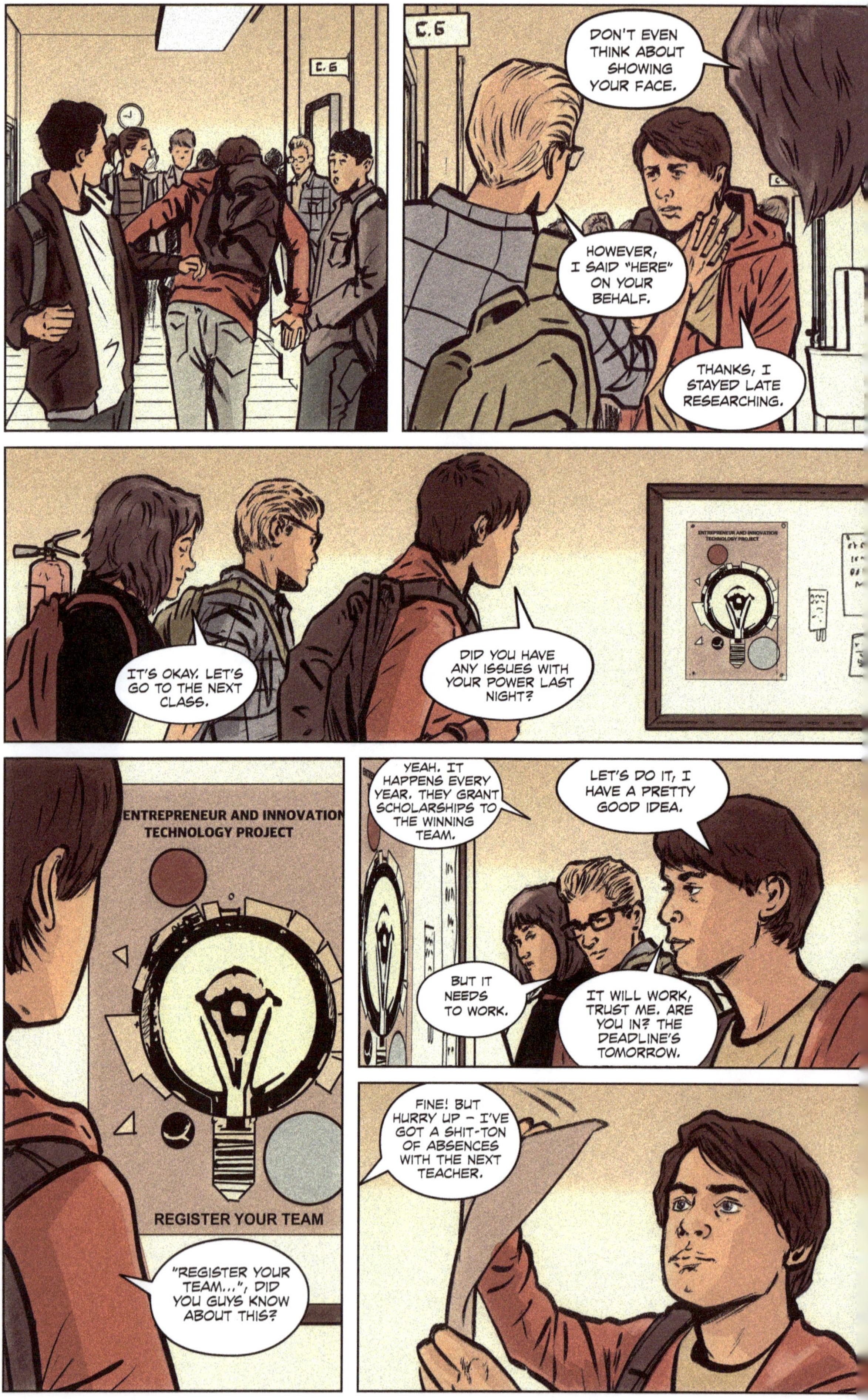
C.6
C.6
DON'T EVEN THINK ABOUT SHOWING YOUR FACE.
HOWEVER, I SAID "HERE" ON YOUR BEHALF.
THANKS, I STAYED LATE RESEARCHING.
IT'S OKAY. LET'S GO TO THE NEXT CLASS.
DID YOU HAVE ANY ISSUES WITH YOUR POWER LAST NIGHT?
ENTREPRENEUR AND INNOVATION TECHNOLOGY PROJECT
REGISTER YOUR TEAM
"REGISTER YOUR TEAM...", DID YOU GUYS KNOW ABOUT THIS?
YEAH. IT HAPPENS EVERY YEAR. THEY GRANT SCHOLARSHIPS TO THE WINNING TEAM.
LET'S DO IT, I HAVE A PRETTY GOOD IDEA.
BUT IT NEEDS TO WORK.
IT WILL WORK, TRUST ME. ARE YOU IN? THE DEADLINE'S TOMORROW.
FINE! BUT HURRY UP - I'VE GOT A SHIT-TON OF ABSENCES WITH THE NEXT TEACHER.

WELLAR! WELLAR!
YES?
DID YOU HEAR ME? YOU NEED TO GO TO PRINCIPAL MILLER'S OFFICE.
AND I THOUGHT THAT HE WAS PAYING ATTENTION.

...DON'T LET THE BRONZE SNAKE...STEAL THE SILVER THREAD...WE DON'T DREAM...WE'RE A FRAGMENTED MEMORY...IT CRYSTALLIZED WITH SOUND... IT HAS TO BE CAUGHT...
GOOD MORNING! SORRY, I GOT CALLED INTO A LAST-MINUTE MEETING.
STOP!

IT'S FINE, I JUST GOT HERE.
ALL RIGHT, HOW HAVE YOU BEEN?
I'VE BEEN FINE, THANKS.
THAT DAY I SAW YOU, YOUR NAME RANG A BELL. I CHECKED YOUR FILE AND FOUND YOU'RE BESSIE'S SON.
DO YOU KNOW HER?
OF COURSE! SHE'S AN OLD FRIEND. THAT'S PROBABLY WHY YOU LOOK FAMILIAR. SMALL WORLD.
WHAT DO YOU THINK ABOUT THE SCHOOL?
IT'S INTERESTING.
I'VE BEEN TOLD YOU'RE VERY BRIGHT; HOWEVER, YOU'VE BEEN ARRIVING LATE TO CLASS.
I'LL WORK ON THAT.
T'S FINE, I'M NOT ALLING YOU OUT. NOT YET, ANYWAY. AVE YOU ALREADY ECIDED ON YOUR MAJOR?
NOT YET, I LIKE NUMBERS, BUT I LIKE ART TOO.
STEP BY STEP. ANY SIDE PROJECT YOU'RE WORKING ON?
I HAVE A FEW IDEAS. MY FRIENDS AND I ARE GOING TO ENTER THE "ENTREPRENEUR AND INNOVATION PROJECT" CONTEST.
AWESOME! WHAT WILL THE PROJECT BE ABOUT?
SORRY. MAY I ASK YOU SOMETHING ELSE?
SURE, GO AHEAD.
IF YOU KNOW MY MOM, THEN, DID YOU HAVE THE CHANCE TO MEET MY DAD?
NOT REALLY. I REMEMBER HE PASSED AWAY IN AN ACCIDENT A FEW YEARS AGO, VERY SORRY. AND CHANGING THE TOPIC: WHAT DID YOU SAY YOUR PROJECT WAS ABOUT?
I DIDN'T, IT'S A DEVICE TO HELP REMEMBER DREAMS.
INTERESTING, LIKE A "DREAMCATCHER"?
KIND OF.
I'M SORRY, BUT I HAVE TO GO. MY MOM'S ALREADY WAITING FOR ME.
TAKE CARE, AND KEEP ME POSTED ON THE PROGRESS.

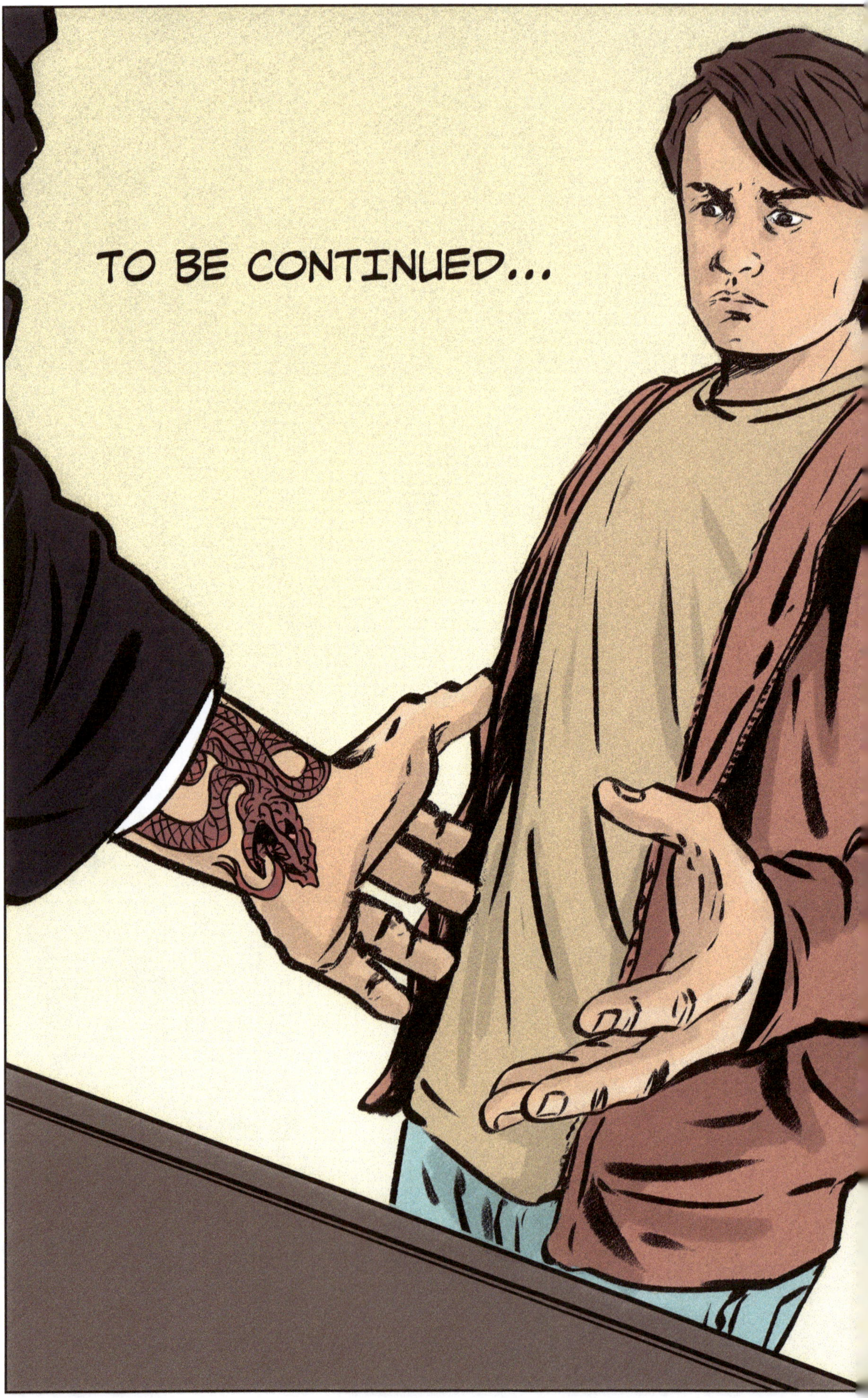
TO BE CONTINUED...

I NEED YOU TO LISTEN TO THIS.
AREN'T YOU GONNA TELL US WHAT THE PRINCIPAL WANTED FIRST?
THIS IS MORE IMPORTANT– EVERYTHING'S CONNECTED.
DOES THAT WORK?
DOES THIS REALLY WORK?
I GUESS IT NEEDS NEW BATTERIES.
WE'LL LISTEN LATER – FIRST, TELL US HOW IT WENT.
I'M CONVINCED IT'S ALL CONNECTED: MY DAD'S ACCIDENT, THE WORD 'OPHIUCHUS', AND DREAMS.
I'M NOT FOLLOWING YOU.
I'LL EXPLAIN IT LATER. I HAVE TO GO HOME TO CHECK ON SOMETHING. SHEP, CAN YOU FINISH SUBMITTING US TO THE CONTEST? ELLA, LOOK FOR PLACES WITH OLD PRINT NEWS ABOUT ACCIDENTS TEN YEARS AGO OR MORE, I'LL RESEARCH "DREAMCATCHERS".
WE HAVE A LOT TO DO!
AND BUY BATTERIES FOR THAT THING!
I SAID BATTERIES!
¿WELLAR?

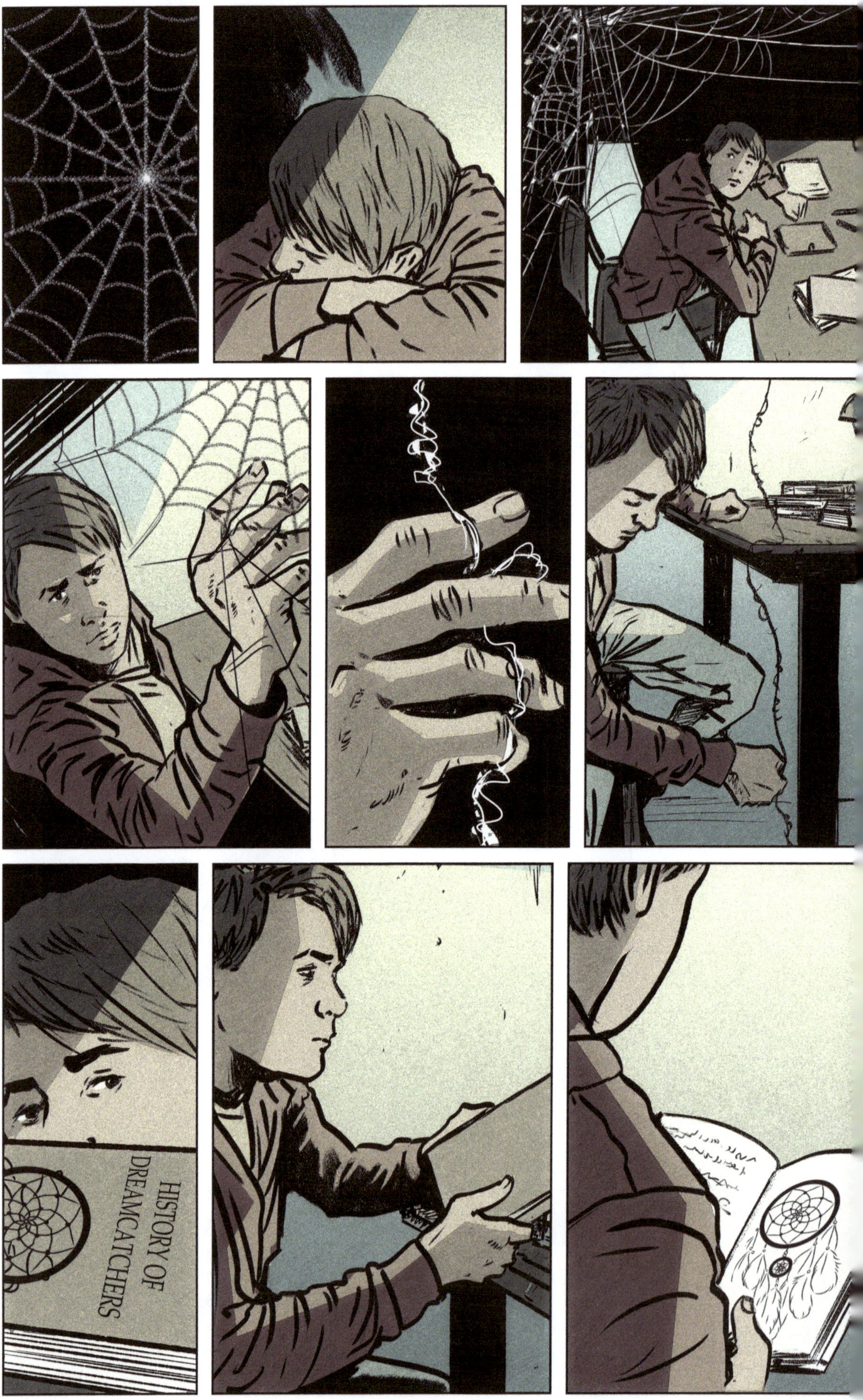
HISTORY OF
DREAMCATCHERS

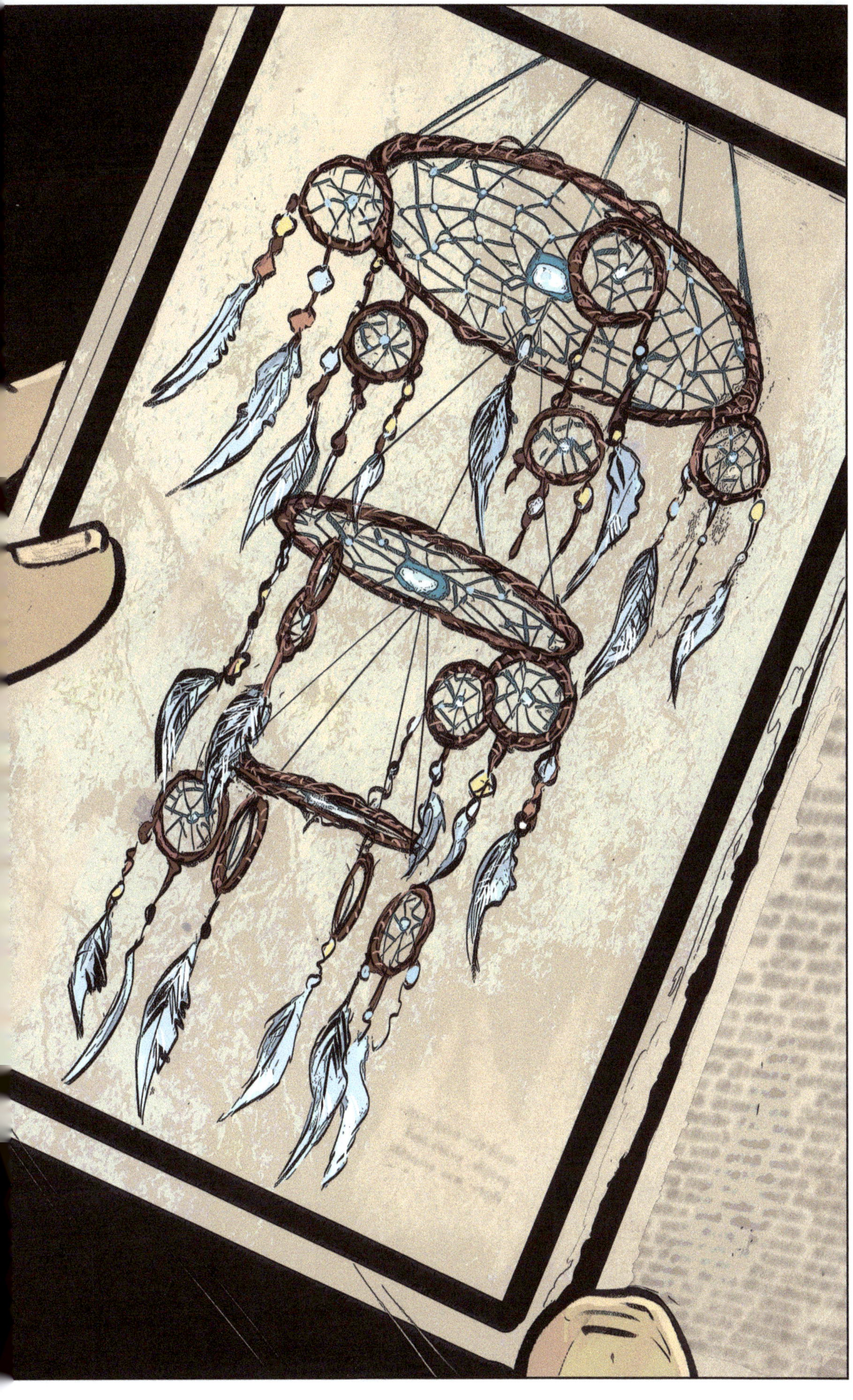

SO BASICALLY IT'S A BIG "DREAMCATCHER" THAT DOES EXACTLY THAT.
YEAH–BASICALLY, IT CATCHES DREAMS.
BUT HOW DO YOU PLAN TO DO THAT?
TESLA SAID THOUGHTS COULD BE PHOTOGRAPHED–I DON'T SEE WHY DREAMS COULDN'T BE.
DID HE DO IT?
WELL...
WELLAR, DON'T TAKE IT THE WRONG WAY, I THINK IT'S A GREAT IDEA, BUT WE NEED TO HAVE A CLEAR PLAN FOR HOW TO DO IT.
I HAVE A COUPLE OF THEORIES.
FOR EXAMPLE?
HAVE YOU HEARD ABOUT THE "SILVER CORD"? IT'S AN ENERGY BOND BETWEEN THE PHYSICAL AND ASTRAL BODIES.
ASTRAL TRAVELS? THAT SOUNDS MORE LIKE MAGIC THAN SCIENCE.
PERHAPS, BUT IT'S A CLUE FROM THE TAPE.
THE TAPE ONLY YOU'VE HEARD?
CLICK

CLACK!
GUYS, PLEASE—QUIET DOWN. PEOPLE ARE TRYING TO STUDY. OTHERWISE, YOU'LL HAVE TO LEAVE.
SORRY, MY FRIEND GOT SOME SHOCKING NEWS.
BY THE WAY, I FOUND A PLACE WHERE WE CAN LOOK FOR INFO ON YOUR DAD'S ACCIDENT. DO YOU WANT TO GO NOW?

ARCHIVE
Second comedy of season to play tonight-Saturday
STREET NEWS
Campus to celebrate heritage week Nov. 14
New buffet luncheon offers soup, salad line
Gazette
COUNTY FAIR A HUGE SUCCESS
FARMING SUPPLIES
BADASS! I DIDN'T KNOW THIS KIND OF STUFF STILL EXISTED.
WAS IT 10 OR 15 YEARS AGO? WE'LL BE HERE FOR A WHILE.
LET'S SAY 13 YEARS.
AND WHY IS ELLA THE ONE DOING ALL THE HEAVY LIFTING HERE?
CAUSE I FOUND IT, DUH. IT'S LIKE A HORROR MOVIE TROPE OR SOMETHING. THE GIRL ALWAYS FINDS THE CLUES.
WELL, BY ACCIDENT OR SOMETHING SIMILAR, I DIDN'T FIND ANYTHING, DO YOU WANT TO TRY SOMETHING ELSE?
WHY DON'T YOU TRY "OBITUARIES" OR "WAKES"? THEY PROBABLY RAN SOMETHING IN THE LOCAL PAPER BACK THEN.
OBITUARIES
SMART MOVE, SHERLOCK!
I THINK I FOUND SOMETHING, FROM 13 YEARS AGO.
HOLD UP!

"THE CAUSE OF THE DEATH HASN'T BEEN RELEASED...THE ONLY STATEMENT SO FAR IS THAT IT WAS A TERRIBLE ACCIDENT..."
CAN YOU ZOOM IN ON THAT PIC?
LET ME SEE.
ISN'T THAT PRINCIPAL MILLER?
IT LOOKS LIKE HIM.
WHEN I TALKED TO HIM, HE SAID HE DIDN'T KNOW MY DAD.
WELL, WE STILL DON'T KNOW IF IT'S YOUR DAD—THERE'S NO NAME ON IT.
I'M WITH SHEP ON THIS ONE, YOU'RE JUMPING TO CONCLUSIONS.
ALL RIGHT, HERE'S WHAT I THINK: PRINCIPAL MILLER IS HIDING SOMETHING, AND I'M SURE IT'S RELATED TO MY DAD'S DEATH.
EVEN IF THAT'S TRUE, WHAT CAN WE REALLY DO ABOUT IT?
WE NEED TO BREAK INTO HIS HOUSE. HE MUST KEEP INFORMATION THERE.
YOU'RE SERIOUS?
ARE YOU KIDDING? I SUCK AT MATH, BUT I'M NOT A CRIMINAL.
WE WON'T STEAL ANYTHING—JUST LOOK AROUND.
"JUST LOOK AROUND"?
IF YOU'RE NOT IN, I'LL GO ALONE.
NO WAY, MAN. THAT'S CRAZY.
HE'S CAPABLE OF GOING ALONE, AND I DON'T KNOW WHAT COULD HAPPEN.

SO, WHAT DO YOU THINK?
LET'S TALK AFTER THE CLASS.

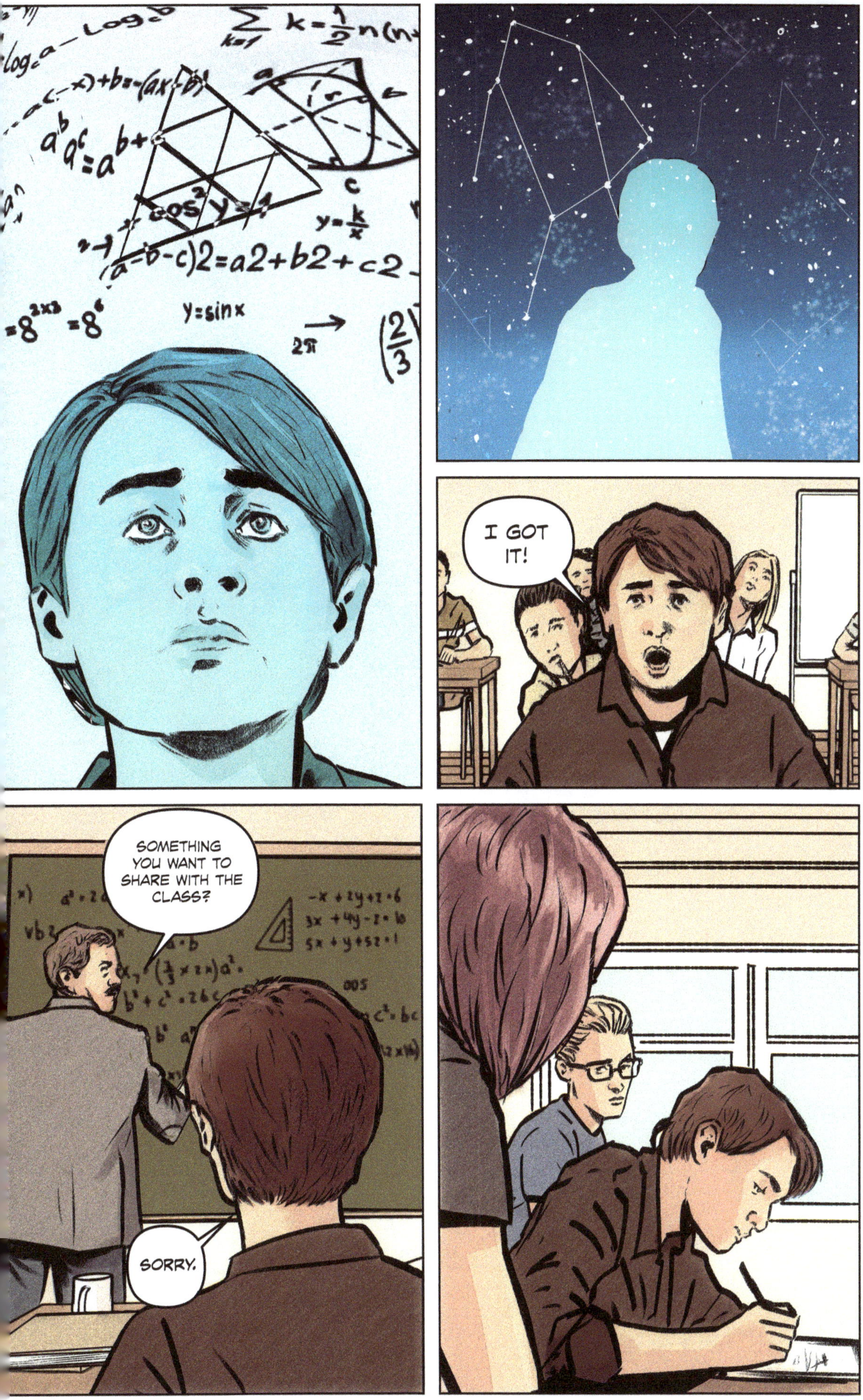
I GOT IT!
SOMETHING YOU WANT TO SHARE WITH THE CLASS?
SORRY.

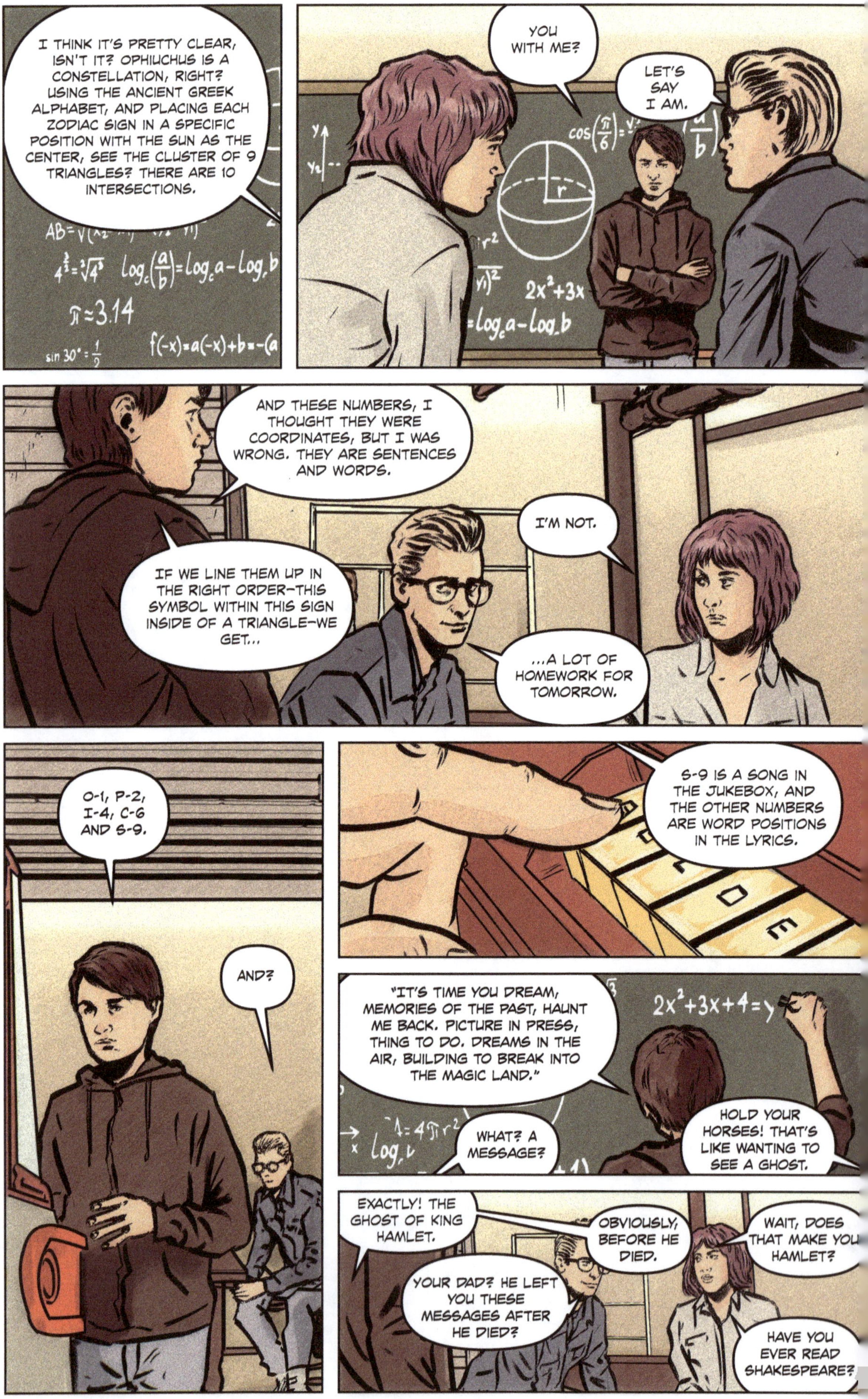
I THINK IT'S PRETTY CLEAR, ISN'T IT? OPHIUCHUS IS A CONSTELLATION, RIGHT? USING THE ANCIENT GREEK ALPHABET, AND PLACING EACH ZODIAC SIGN IN A SPECIFIC POSITION WITH THE SUN AS THE CENTER, SEE THE CLUSTER OF 9 TRIANGLES? THERE ARE 10 INTERSECTIONS.
YOU WITH ME?
LET'S SAY I AM.
AND THESE NUMBERS, I THOUGHT THEY WERE COORDINATES, BUT I WAS WRONG. THEY ARE SENTENCES AND WORDS.
IF WE LINE THEM UP IN THE RIGHT ORDER—THIS SYMBOL WITHIN THIS SIGN INSIDE OF A TRIANGLE—WE GET...
I'M NOT.
...A LOT OF HOMEWORK FOR TOMORROW.
O-1, P-2, I-4, C-6 AND S-9.
AND?
S-9 IS A SONG IN THE JUKEBOX, AND THE OTHER NUMBERS ARE WORD POSITIONS IN THE LYRICS.
"IT'S TIME YOU DREAM, MEMORIES OF THE PAST, HAUNT ME BACK. PICTURE IN PRESS, THING TO DO. DREAMS IN THE AIR, BUILDING TO BREAK INTO THE MAGIC LAND."
WHAT? A MESSAGE?
HOLD YOUR HORSES! THAT'S LIKE WANTING TO SEE A GHOST.
EXACTLY! THE GHOST OF KING HAMLET.
YOUR DAD? HE LEFT YOU THESE MESSAGES AFTER HE DIED?
OBVIOUSLY, BEFORE HE DIED.
WAIT, DOES THAT MAKE YOU HAMLET?
HAVE YOU EVER READ SHAKESPEARE?

NOPE, BUT I WATCHED THE MOVIE WITH LAURENE OLIVIER. SO WHO AM I? HORATIO? AND YOU'RE OPHELIA?
DON'T MESS WITH ME! I DON'T KNOW WHO SHE IS.
DO YOU SEE IT? OR ARE YOU JUST MESSING WITH ME?
TAKE IT EASY BRO. IT'S NOT THAT WE DON'T BELIEVE YOU, IT'S JUST A LOT TO TAKE IN.
SHEP IS RIGHT, BUT LET'S SAY THAT IT ALL MAKES SENSE, WHAT IS THE MESSAGE?
I NEED TO BUILD SOMETHING TO CATCH MY DREAMS AND FIND OUT WHAT REALLY HAPPENED TO MY DAD'S MEMORIES.
IF THAT'S WHAT YOU WANT, I'M DOWN!
ME TOO! BUT WHAT WAS THAT ABOUT THE "MAGIC LAND"?
THANK YOU! BUT THERE'S ONE MORE ISSUE. IF I PLAY ALL THE SONGS IN A CERTAIN ORDER, A NON-REGISTERED OPTION IS ACTIVATED—BUT THE DISK IS BROKEN, AND I ONLY FOUND A PIECE...
...AND THE HOMEWORK WITH THE PROBLEM SOLVED IS RIGHT THERE ON THE BOARD...
AND FOR THE RECORD, THAT DOESN'T MAKE ME THAT SO-CALLED OPHELIA. CLEAR?
I OWE YOU THE KISS BRO. SEE YOU EARLY TOMORROW!
did you ever have a dream thrill you with, "will you be mine?"
DID YOU EVER SEE A DREAM WALKING

did you ever see a dream walking?
BEEP
BEEP
BEEP
BEEEEP
BEEP
BEEEEP
TAXI
I DON'T KNOW HOW YOU CAN CONCENTRATE WITH ALL THIS NOISE.
HOW'S THE PROJECT GOING?
I ASKED ABOUT YOUR PROJECT— HOW'S IT GOING?
CLICK!
SORRY, IT'S GOING WELL.
IS THAT ALL YOU HAVE TO REPORT?
EXCUSE ME?
NEVER MIND.
CLICK!

BEEP
WHY AREN'T THEY MOVING?
IT'S FINE MOM, I CAN WALK FROM HERE, IT ISN'T THAT FAR.
NO, WAIT.
GOOD LUCK! I LOVE YOU!

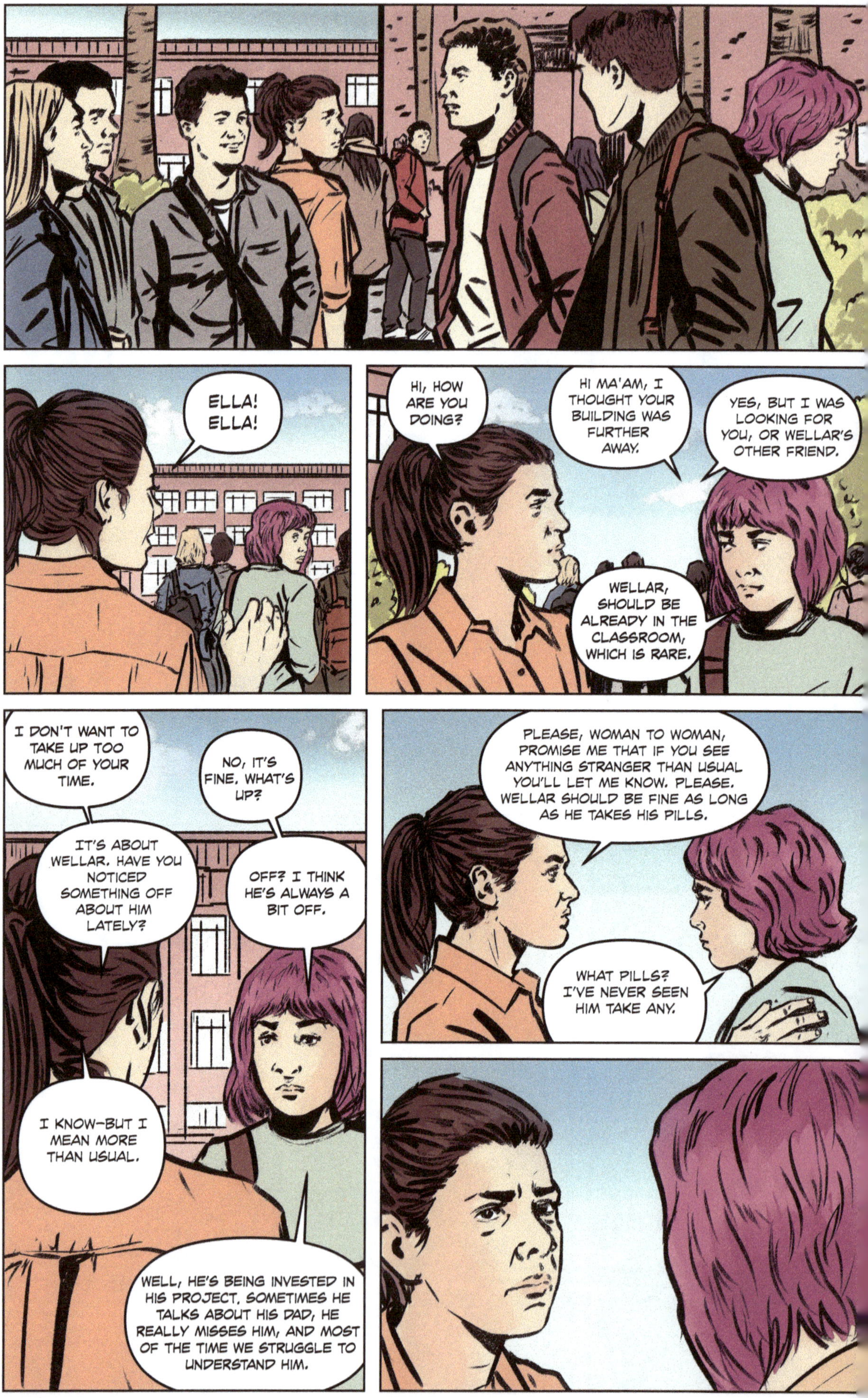
ELLA! ELLA!
HI, HOW ARE YOU DOING?
HI MA'AM, I THOUGHT YOUR BUILDING WAS FURTHER AWAY.
YES, BUT I WAS LOOKING FOR YOU, OR WELLAR'S OTHER FRIEND.
WELLAR, SHOULD BE ALREADY IN THE CLASSROOM, WHICH IS RARE.
I DON'T WANT TO TAKE UP TOO MUCH OF YOUR TIME.
NO, IT'S FINE. WHAT'S UP?
IT'S ABOUT WELLAR. HAVE YOU NOTICED SOMETHING OFF ABOUT HIM LATELY?
OFF? I THINK HE'S ALWAYS A BIT OFF.
I KNOW—BUT I MEAN MORE THAN USUAL.
WELL, HE'S BEING INVESTED IN HIS PROJECT, SOMETIMES HE TALKS ABOUT HIS DAD, HE REALLY MISSES HIM, AND MOST OF THE TIME WE STRUGGLE TO UNDERSTAND HIM.
PLEASE, WOMAN TO WOMAN, PROMISE ME THAT IF YOU SEE ANYTHING STRANGER THAN USUAL YOU'LL LET ME KNOW. PLEASE. WELLAR SHOULD BE FINE AS LONG AS HE TAKES HIS PILLS.
WHAT PILLS? I'VE NEVER SEEN HIM TAKE ANY.

WELL, AT LEAST NOT IN FRONT OF ME. HE PROBABLY DOESN'T WANT US TO SEE HIM TAKING PILLS, DID I SAY SOMETHING WRONG?
NO, AND THANK YOU.
WAS THAT WELLAR'S MOM?
HAVE YOU SEEN HIM TAKING PILLS?
LIKE METH? THAT WOULD EXPLAIN A LOT.
NO DUMBASS, MEDICATION!
I HAVE NOT, BUT HURRY UP WE'RE LATE.

THIS ONE'S ABOUT "DREAM CATCHERS", THIS ONE'S "CRYSTALS AND QUARTZ", "ENERGY MEASUREMENTS", "TESLA COILS". WHAT ELSE? I THINK IT'S A GOOD START.
BESIDES SHOWING US THE BOOKS, IS THERE SOMETHING ELSE YOU WANT TO TALK ABOUT?
YOUR MOM CAME TO TALK TO ME THIS MORNING.
WHAT DID SHE WANT?
SHE ASKED ME ABOUT THE MEDICATION YOU SUPPOSEDLY SHOULD BE TAKING.
IS THAT IT?
WELLAR, I DON'T WANT TO GET IN TROUBLE.
NO, DON'T WORRY. IT'S NOTHING.
ALL RIGHT, I NEED YOUR HELP TO BREAK INTO THE PRINCIPAL MILLER'S HOUSE.
AGAIN WITH THAT?
HE MUST BE HIDING INFORMATION ABOUT MY DAD AND WHAT HE WAS DOING.
WHAT IF HE'S ONLY A SAD OLD MAN WITH A BAD MEMORY?
YOU DON'T HAVE TO GO IN, I JUST WANT TO KNOW IF YOU'RE DOWN OR NOT.
OK, I'M DOWN, BUT YOU NEED TO BE VERY SPECIFIC ON WHAT YOU NEED.
I'M NOT FULLY CONVINCED, BUT IF I LEAVE YOU TWO ALONE, YOU'LL MESS IT UP.
THANK YOU, GUYS!
DON'T GET TOO CORNY.
WELL, WHAT DO YOU NEED, AND WHEN?
TODAY.
NO BULLSHIT!
SHHHH!

HAVE YOU SEEN HEIST MOVIES? IT TAKES THEM A WHILE TO PUT TOGETHER A SOLID PLAN.
WE DON'T HAVE THAT MUCH TIME. WHAT IF HE GETS RID OF THE INFORMATION?
BUT, AS SHEP SAID, WHAT DO YOU NEED? AND WHAT INFORMATION ARE YOU TALKING ABOUT?
AS MUCH AS POSSIBLE ABOUT MILLER: HIS ADDRESS, SCHEDULE, ETC.
YOU MAY BE A BIG DEAL WITH NUMBERS, BUT FINDING INFORMATION IS MY THING.
BUT WHAT AM I GOING TO DO?
YOU'RE OUR SECRET WEAPON.
DUMBASS!
HE DOESN'T HAVE "FACE" NOR "INSTA", BUT I THINK I GOT IT: I KNOW HIS ADDRESS, NOT FAR FROM HERE. WIDOWER. AND TODAY'S THE ONLY DAY HE TEACHES THE NIGHT SHIFT.
AM I THE REAL DEAL OR WHAT? STILL, IT'S ODD, HE'S BEEN PRINCIPAL HERE FOR THE LAST 13 YEARS, AND BEFORE THAT THERE'S NOTHING ABOUT HIM. NOTHING AT ALL.
AWESOME! I'LL TELL MOM I'M STAYING AT YOUR PLACE TO STUDY.
AND WHAT AM I GOING TO DO?
HOLD UP, AND HOW DO YOU PLAN TO GET IN?
I'M PRETTY GOOD AT OPENING DOORS. AT THE END OF THE DAY IT'S A SIMPLE MECHANISM.
YOU'LL NEED MY HELP, THOUGH, MORE THAN LIKELY IT'LL HAVE AN ALARM, LIKE MOST OF THE HOUSES AROUND HERE.
AND WHAT DO YOU KNOW ABOUT ALARMS?
HIS DAD OWNS THE ONLY ALARM COMPANY IN THIS AREA.
AND I KNOW EVERYTHING ABOUT HACKING THESE DEVICES, WELL, IN THEORY.
BUT...
I'M YOUR ONLY OPTION. YOU HAVE NO IDEA HOW IT WORKS.
BUT, WHAT AM I GOING TO DO?
YOU'LL KEEP LOOKOUT ON MILLER AND KEEP US POSTED.
TO BE HONEST, IT SOUNDS VERY HAPHAZARD, BUT...
IT IS WHAT IT IS.

MOM, WE'LL GO TO SHEP'S HOUSE. WE HAVE AN EXAM TOMORROW. IS THAT OKAY?
EXAM? YOU DIDN'T TELL ME ANYTHING ABOUT IT, AND WHY DON'T YOU GO AND STUDY AT HOME?
I HAVE TO BE AT HOME MY PARENTS ARE OUT OF TOWN AND I HAVE TO FEED THE CAT.
RIGHT?
YOU'D BETTER NOT BE LYING. AND STAY OUT OF TROUBLE, OKAY?
DON'T WORRY, SEE YOU TONIGHT.
AND HOW ARE YOU GETTING BACK HOME?
I'LL TAKE A CAB.

DO YOU REALLY HAVE A CAT?
DID YOU SEE THE LOOK ON YOUR MOM'S FACE? SHE'LL EAT ME ALIVE IF SOMETHING HAPPENS TO YOU.
NOTHING WILL HAPPEN TO ME, "THAT IF YOU BE HONEST AND FAIR, YOUR HONESTY SHOULD ADMIT NO DISCOURSE TO YOUR BEAUTY".
DON'T START WITH YOUR STUFF.
HOLD ON, YOU SCUMBAGS!

WE ARE ALMOST IN FRONT OF THE HOUSE, WHAT'S THE LATEST?
HE'S STILL IN HIS OFFICE, HE'S ON THE PHONE WITH SOMEONE.
OK, LET US KNOW IF SOMETHING HAPPENS.

AND DO YOU REALLY KNOW HOW TO DO IT?
YOUR TURN.
CLICK
RING RING RING
4-7-5-1-6
DO YOU HAVE ANY IDEA OF WHAT WE'RE LOOKING FOR?
I'LL KNOW WHEN I FIND IT.

YES! YES! I KNOW, YOU'VE REPEATED IT A MILLION TIMES! BUT HE'S JUST A KID, AND I DON'T WANT ANYTHING TO DO WITH IT. AND YES, I'M WELL AWARE OF THE CONSEQUENCES—I DON'T NEED TO HEAR YOUR THREATS AGAIN!
MILLER IS GOING TO HIS CLASS.
I'M SURE THERE'S SOMETHING HIDDEN.
WE'VE ALREADY LOOKED EVERYWHERE. MAYBE IT'S SOMEWHERE ELSE, LIKE A STORAGE UNIT.

FOR THE NEXT CLASS, REVIEW THE BUSINESS CASE AND EXPLAIN WHY YOU'D MAKE A DIFFERENT DECISION. YOU CAN DO IT IN CLASS OR AS HOMEWORK. I'M GOING TO HAVE TO LEAVE.
MILLER! MILLER!
PRINCIPAL! GOOD EVENING!
WHAT CAN I DO FOR YOU?
WELL, THE THING IS I'M STILL UNDECIDED ON MY MAJOR, AND I'D LIKE YOUR OPINION.
I CAN'T RIGHT NOW. PLEASE COME TO MY OFFICE TOMORROW MORNING.
BUT I'M GOING TO BE OUT OF TOWN THE ENTIRE WEEK, AND MY PARENTS HAVE BEEN ASKING ME ABOUT IT.
OKAY, WHAT DO YOU WANT TO KNOW?
MILLER IS OMING, WE NEED TO GO OUT.
GIVE ME A MINUTE.
NOW!
I SAID A MINUTE!

CLICK
CRYSTALIZED!
TO BE CONTINUED...

Orion
Ursa Major

...YEAH, I KINDA LIKE NUMBERS, BUT I DON'T KNOW, MAYBE CHEMISTRY?
THE ONLY THING I CAN SAY IS, 'THIS, ABOVE ALL: TO THINE OWN SELF BE TRUE'.
GUYS, MILLER´S HEADING HOME, GET UR ASSES OUT!
HE'S ON THE WAY. LET'S HEAD OUT.
WAIT FOR ME OUTSIDE!

THIS IS BAD—MILLER JUST GOT HERE AND WELLAR'S STILL INSIDE.
CLICK
brr
brr
brr
brr
brr
brr

WHERE'S WELLAR?
STILL INSIDE.
GO KNOCK. DISTRACT HIM.
WHY ME?

NOOOOOO!

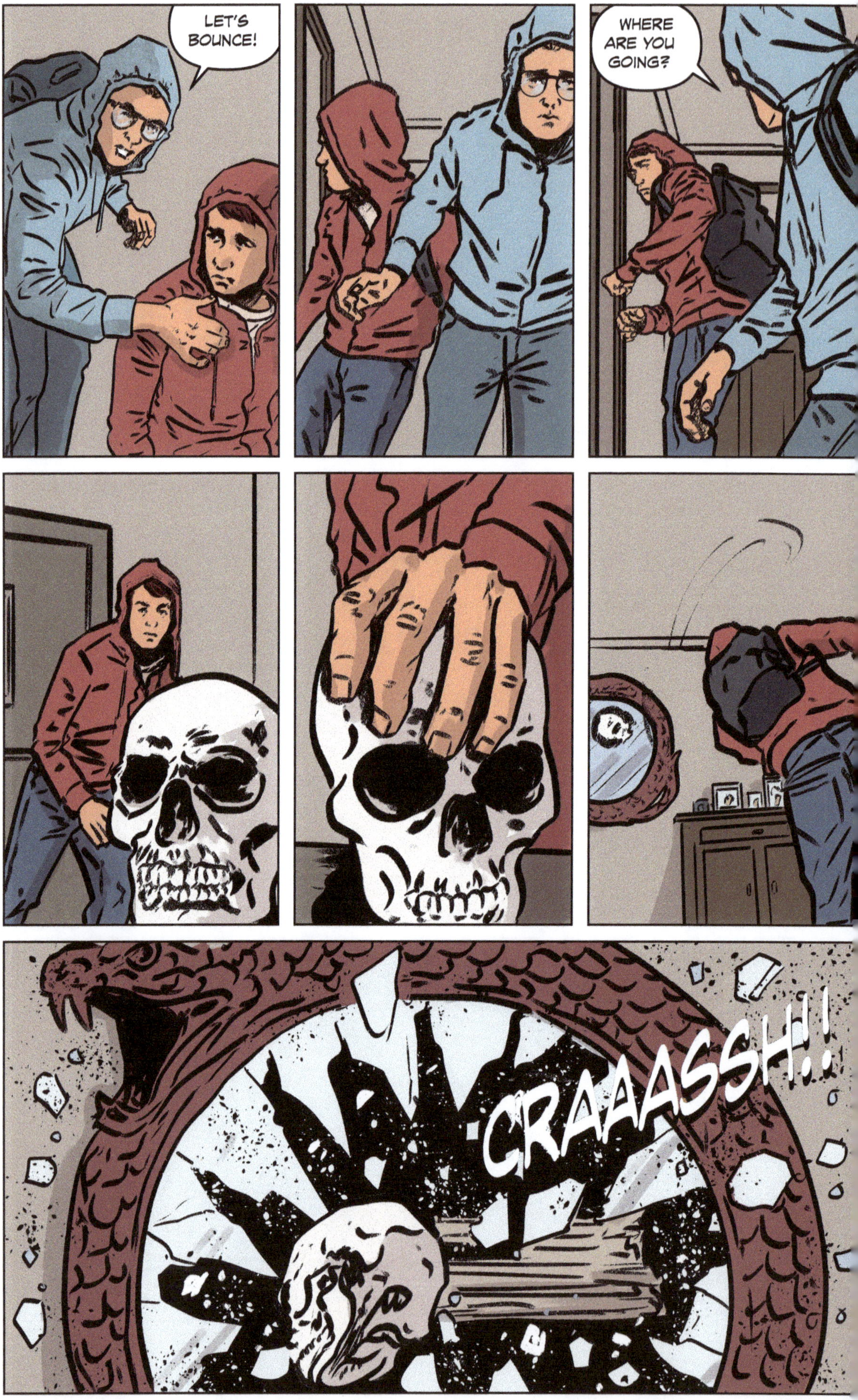
LET'S BOUNCE!
WHERE ARE YOU GOING?
CRAAASSH!!

MOM! I GOTTA TELL YOU SOMETHING REAL—
JUST IN TIME FOR DINNER. AND WE HAVE COMPANY.
GOOD EVENING, WELLAR.
WE AGREED ON TWO WEEKS, BUT I THOUGHT IT'D BE A GOOD CHANCE TO TALK.
AND I THINK IT'S A GREAT IDEA. HAND OVER YOUR BACKPACK SO YOU CAN RELAX.
NO!
DON'T BE RIDICULOUS.

WHY DON'T YOU TAKE FLETCHER TO THE BASEMENT AND SHOW HIM YOUR PROGRESS ON THE PROJECT?
ONLY IF WELLAR'S OKAY WITH THAT.
COME ON, OF COURSE HE WANTS TO. DINNER'S NOT QUITE READY YET.

INTERESTING!
IS THIS THE FAMOUS PROJECT? AND WHAT'D YOU SAY IT WAS FOR?
I HAVEN'T SAID.
WELLAR, DO YOU KNOW WHY I'M HERE?
I GUESS YOU'RE ABOUT TO TELL ME.
YOUR MOM'S WORRIED. SHE'S NOT SURE THIS MOVE WAS A GOOD IDEA.
I'VE JUST BEEN REALLY BUSY...
...AND SHE SUSPECTS YOU'VE STOPPED TAKING YOUR MEDS.
MAYBE I'VE MISSED A COUPLE...
AND THIS BEAUTY?

HAVE A LITTLE DREAM OF ME
“Everything
we touch will turn to clover
In the magic land
of what's
YOU STILL WANNA STAY HERE AND PRESENT YOUR PROJECT? I'M HONESTLY PRETTY CURIOUS TO SEE HOW IT WORKS.
DINNER'S READY!

DELICIOUS. AS ALWAYS, YOUR COOKING NEVER DISAPPOINTS.
THANK YOU! DID YOU SEE WHAT WELLAR'S BUILDING? IT LOOKS INCREDIBLE—HAS HE TOLD YOU WHAT IT'S FOR?
YEAH, I SAW IT, BUT NOT MANY DETAILS YET.
THOUGHT SO. IT'S A MACHINE TO RECALL DREAMS. DON'T ASK ME HOW, BUT IT SOUNDS AMAZING.
MOM, DID YOU KNOW THE DOCTOR AND DAD ALSO SHARE A LOVE FOR JAZZ?
"SHE'S SO TANGLED IN MY LIFE AND SOUL..."
THAT LIKE THE STAR, SHE MOVES NOT EXCEPT IN HER SPHERE."
PLEASE, NO MORE HAMLET AT DINNER. TEACHING IT ALL DAY IS ENOUGH.
"THE SERPENT THAT POISONED YOUR FATHER'S LIFE NOW WEARS HIS CROWN."
WELLAR!
EXCUSE ME FOR A MOMENT.

WHY DO YOU ALWAYS HAVE TO ACT LIKE THIS?
SORRY, SOMETHING URGENT CAME UP.
DON'T WORRY. THANKS FOR COMING.
UNTIL NEXT TIME. GOOD LUCK ON YOUR PRESENTATION, WELLAR. HOPE IT GOES GREAT.
THOK!
HE TOOK STUFF FROM MY BACKPACK!
WHAT DO YOU THINK HE TOOK?
DOCS, PHOTOS, AND A PIECE OF A RECORD.
A RECORD? WELLAR, YOU CAN'T JUST ACCUSE SOMEONE OF THEFT LIKE THAT.
YOU DON'T GET IT!

HERE IT IS!
PRESTIGIOUS SCHOOL DIRECTOR FOUND DEAD HIS MORNING IN HIS OME. SIGNS POINT TO RAGIC ACCIDENT THAT...
THAT WASN'T AN "ACCIDENT".
LOOK, I JUST SAW HIM LYING THERE, I'M NOT EVEN SURE WHAT HAPPENED.
ME NEITHER, BUT HE WAS DEFINITELY OFF. ARGUING ON THE PHONE WITH SOMEONE.
IT'S CLEAR, HE DIDN'T AGREE WITH THEM, AND THEY GOT RID OF HIM.
WHO ARE THEY, "EXACTLY"?
THAT'S WHY DOCTOR FLETCHER CAME OVER LAST NIGHT.
WAIT A MINUTE! WHO'S THAT DOCTOR?
AND HE STOLE THE DOCUMENTS I FOUND.
WHAT DOCUMENTS?

AND TOLD ME SOMETHING ABOUT "BEING TRUE TO MYSELF."
WHAT DID YOU SAY?
WHEN DID YOU BUY A PHONE?
OKAY BUT, WHAT'S UP WITH THE "PROJECT"? IT'S DUE IN TWO DAYS.
TWO DAYS IS ALL I NEED. I'VE GOT IT RIGHT HERE.
WHAT DO YOU THINK, SHEP?
I THINK THIS ALL FEELS LIKE A BAD DREAM.

HAMLET
DIDN'T WANNA WAKE YOU. BUT YOU BETTER SLEEP IN YOUR ROOM.
YEAH, I WAS JUST READING A BIT.
GUESS YOU HEARD ABOUT DIRECTOR MILLER'S ACCIDENT.
UCLA
IT WASN'T AN ACCIDENT.
WHY DO YOU KEEP SAYING STUFF LIKE THAT?
BECAUSE I WAS THERE.
WELLAR, PLEASE.

AND WHAT ARE YOU DOING WITH THAT PHONE?
I TOOK IT FROM MILLER'S HOUSE THAT NIGHT. COULDN'T UNLOCK IT, BUT ELLA GAVE ME A CLUE, "THIS, ABOVE ALL: TO THINE OWN SELF BE TRUE." ACT 1, SCENE 3, LINE 78. CALL THE LAST DIALED NUMBER.
UCLA
I'M NOT PLAYING THIS GAME.
JUST DIAL THE DAMN NUMBER!
DON'T RAISE YOUR VOICE AT ME!
UCLA
NOW I GET WHY YOU STILL BELIEVE DAD'S DEATH WAS JUST AN "ACCIDENT."
PLAF!
UCLA
UCLA
UCLA

HELLO?
FLETCHER? SORRY TO CALL SO LATE.
NO NEED TO APOLOGIZE. IS SOMETHING WRONG WITH WELLAR?
CRACK
HE'S ACTING STRANGE–SAYING WEIRD THINGS.
LIKE WHAT?
THAT YOU STOLE SOME DOCUMENTS AND THAT HE SAW HOW MILLER DIED. I THINK HE'S SLIPPING BACK INTO HIS FANTASY AGAIN.
UNFORTUNATELY, THAT WAS ALWAYS A RISK. IS HE STILL ASKING ABOUT HIS DAD'S ACCIDENT?
YES, BUT I'VE BEEN CHANGING THE SUBJECT LIKE YOU SAID.

WHAT'S HE DOING NOW?
PREPPING FOR HIS PROJECT PRESENTATION. HE'S BEEN IN THE BASEMENT ALL DAY.
AVOID ANOTHER INCIDENT, BEST GIVE HIM SPACE. HAVE HIM TAKE THE MEDS I DROPPED OFF YESTERDAY, AS SOON AS POSSIBLE...WITHOUT HIM KNOWING.
IF YOU THINK THAT'S BEST.
THANKS FOR TELLING ME. YOU DID THE RIGHT THING.
HAMLET
UCLA

YOU GOT EVERYTHING?
VHS TAPES GAVE US SOME TROUBLE.
NOW WE JUST FOLLOW THE INSTRUCTIONS.
SO HOW EXACTLY DOES IT WORK?

IF DREAMS ARE PORTALS TO ALTERNATE REALITIES—REMEMBER THE SILVER THREAD I TOLD YOU ABOUT?
KIND OF—EXPLAIN IT AGAIN.
IT'S WHAT LINKS YOUR PHYSICAL BODY TO YOUR ASTRAL SELF, LETTING YOU TRAVEL BETWEEN THE TWO PLANES.
IT ALSO TRANSFERS INFORMATION AND MEMORIES BETWEEN THEM.
THAT MEANS ANYTHING YOU LEARN OR EXPERIENCE WHILE DREAMING CAN BE REMEMBERED.
WE JUST HAVE TO CAPTURE THAT INFO WHEN THE ASTRAL BODY RETURNS, DECODE THE MESSAGE, AND PRINT THE IMAGES AND SOUNDS TO TAPE.
I THOUGHT IT'D BE WAY MORE COMPLICATED.
THEN LET'S DO THIS!

STRUCTURE
WEB

CRYSTALS
POWER

STOP
REC
PLAY
KPOWW!!
HOLY SH*T!
STILL NOT WORKING?
SOMETHING'S MISSING—AND I DON'T KNOW WHAT.
IF IT DOESN'T WORK, IT DOESN'T. WE'LL GET OTHER CHANCES.
IT HAS TO WORK—THERE'S SOMETHING I'M NOT SEEING.
WELL, WE GOTTA BE THERE BEFORE 10 A.M. OR WE'RE DISQUALIFIED.

ASSUMING IT WORKS... HOW ARE YOU GONNA TEST IT?
YOU MEAN WITH WHO.
THUMMM!!
VCR-DARK

TO BE CONTINUED...

Ursa Major

BONUS TRACK

How to Catch a Dream

Interviews and pictures in the press *
What a way to speak on twenty bucks a week
Don't forget that Rockefeller started out on less

Everything we touch will turn to clover
In the magic land of what's to be *
But until your baby puts it over
Investigar Baby, have a little dream on me

Yes
Well, all right then

Everything we touch will turn to clover
In the magic land of what's to be
Till your daddy puts it over, skip it
Baby, have a dream on me, yes

B5

I'm waltzing in a dream with you [redacted] *
Won't you make the dream come true love?
Hold me to your heart and [redacted]r let me free, *
Always be close to me.

Won't you fill this night with splendor
With your kisses sweet and tender?
Let me hear you whisper "I surrender!",
While I'm waltzing in a dream with you.

12/11

Cover Issue # 1

9:08

How to Catch a Dream

The journey of a thousand miles
begins with a single step.

• *Lao Tzu* •

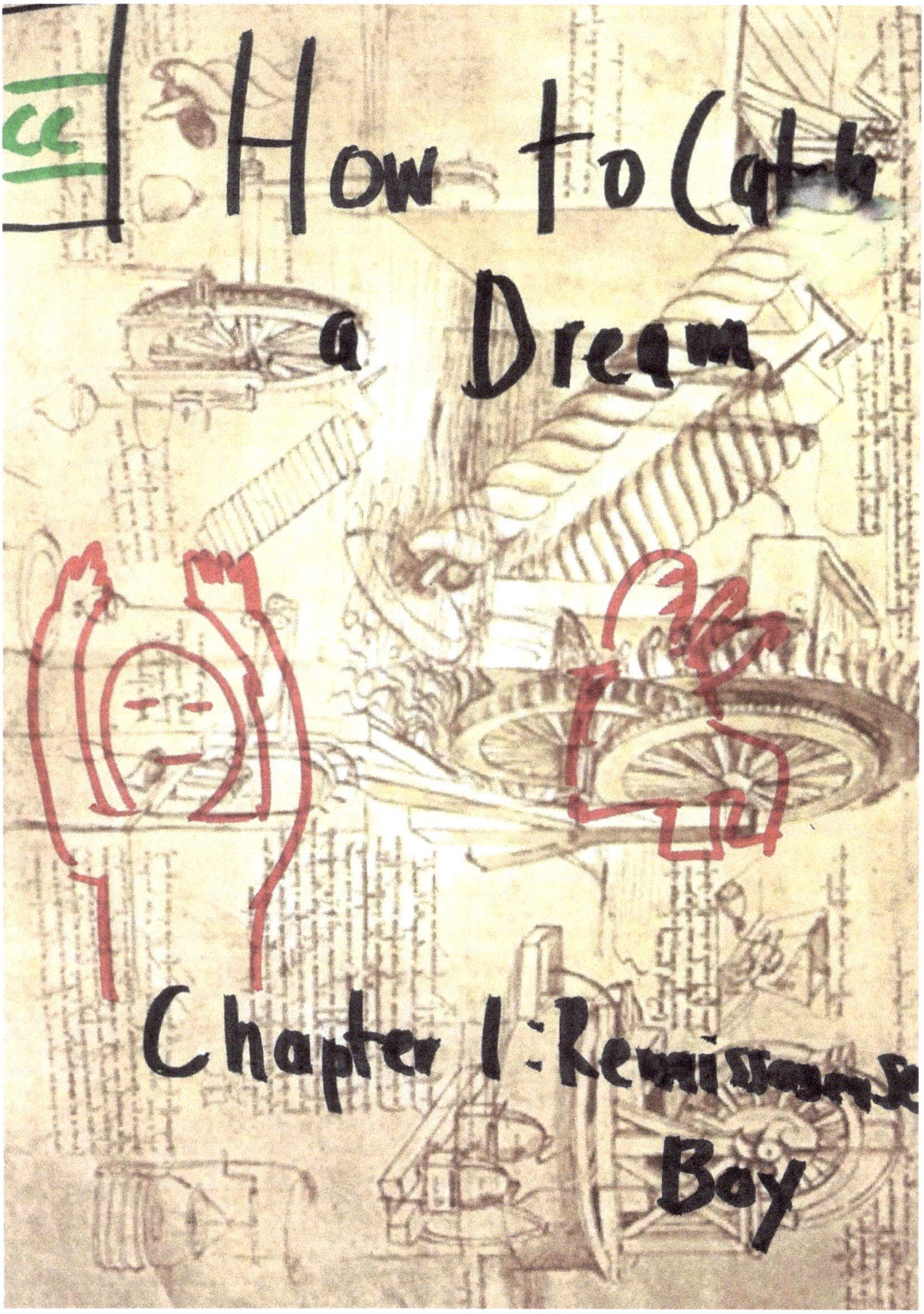
How to Catch a Dream
Chapter 1: Renaissance Boy

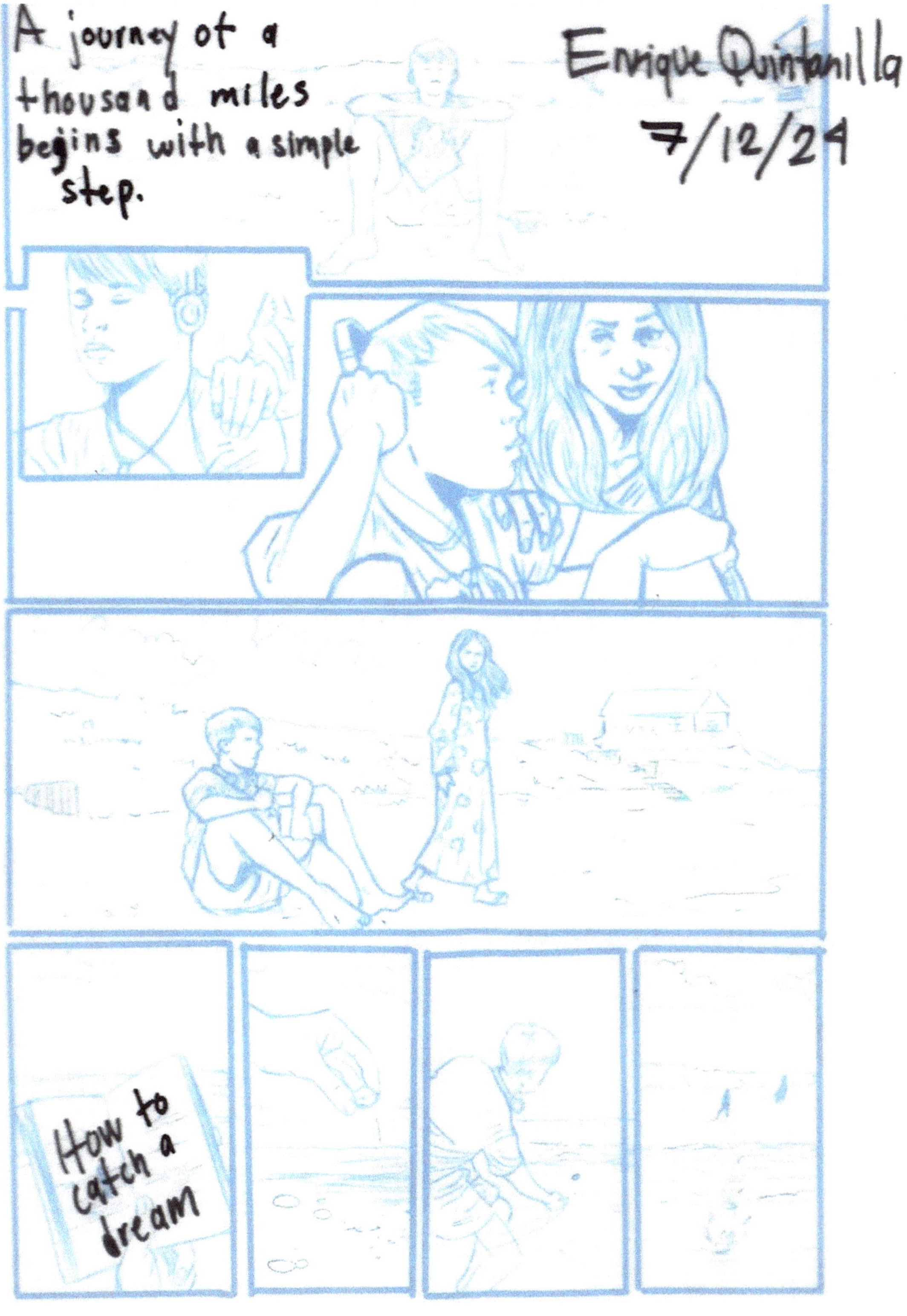
A journey of a thousand miles begins with a simple step.
Enrique Quintanilla
7/12/24
How to catch a dream